PLAYING AFTER DARK

Playing
After Dark

BARBARA LAZEAR ASCHER

PERENNIAL LIBRARY

Harper & Row, Publishers, New York
Cambridge, Philadelphia, San Francisco, Washington
London, Mexico City, São Paulo, Singapore, Sydney

Many of the pieces included in this book originally appeared in various publications, some in a slightly different form and some under a different title.

The following pieces originally appeared in *The New York Times*: "Infidelity," "What Happened to Cynthia Koestler?," "The Obdurate Attender," "The Bag Lady," "On the Road with the College Applicant," "No Girls Allowed (and This Means You!)," " Middle Age: Becoming the Person You always Were."

"Hera and the Workplace" appeared in *Vogue*.

"Mothers and Sons" appeared in *Redbook*

"Caution! Danger Ahead!" appeared in *McCall's*

"If a Bomb is Dropped on Pomfret, Your Desks Will Save You" appeared in *Newsday*.

"A Visit with Eudora Welty" appeared in the *Yale Review* and the *Saturday Review*.

A hardcover edition of this book is published by Doubleday & Company, Inc. It is here reprinted by arrangement with Doubleday & Company, Inc.

First PERENNIAL LIBRARY edition published 1987.

LIBRARY OF CONGRESS CATALOG CARD NUMBER: 87-45019
ISBN: 0-06-097112-6

87 88 89 90 91   MPC 10 9 8 7 6 5 4 3 2 1

For Bob
For Rebecca

Contents

Some Thoughts on Love

Infidelity

Well, I can tell you what I'd do if I discovered that my husband was having a love affair. I'd go get a gun. None of the pertinent information would filter through the buzzing sound that fills the brain when the heart is hurt. I would forget the facts: that I adore him, that there's a family to consider, that he makes a better living than I, that criminal lawyers are expensive. The possibility of widowhood, poverty or prison would not deter. Infidelity is reason enough for strict gun control.

It's hearts like mine that have put laws on the books and the question in the minds of judges and juries: "Is infidelity sufficient provocation to reduce a charge of murder to manslaughter?" Yes, according to eighteenth-century case law, if the killer commits the act "in the first transport of passion." Yes, according to the 1977 English case of *Mossa* v. *the Queen,* if the defendant has been told by his wife, "I've had intercourse with every man on the street" and then throws a telephone at him. Yes, said the law of New Mexico in 1963, it is a complete defense if the accused witnessed the adulterous act. How the defendant would prove this was left to our imaginations (which is probably why the law was repealed in 1973).

I realize that there are people who appear to act rationally in the face of infidelity. Most of them exist in nineteenth- and early twentieth-century fiction. Consider Maggie in Henry James's *The Golden Bowl.* Upon learning that her husband, the prince, was romantically involved with her best friend, who was also her stepmother, she devised a plan that was a work of art. Arms negotiations could not match the complexity of bringing Maggie's husband back to her. It worked, but it seemed to take forever. Few of our hearts are strong enough to cling to flotsam that long—to wait for the whim of current to carry us back to shore.

Consider Leonora, the wife of Edward Ashburnham in Ford Madox Ford's *The Good Soldier.* She facilitated her husband's known infidelities by keeping the object of his affections close at hand. "I suppose," muses Ford's narrator, "that Leonora was pimping for Edward."

Models of restraint. But the lady from Oklahoma wins my admiration. The year was 1927, Manhattan was a long train ride from Tulsa and there were three little children playing about her knees when her sister-in-law approached with grave news. Her husband, the father of these children, was keeping company in New York with a certain actress. Our young mother sent the children off with their aunt and took the next train east. She went to his hotel, and finding him in the dining room in the company of the alleged mistress, she stood before the entire crowd of diners and announced: "Samuel, you are either coming home with me immediately, or you are never coming home again. You are either raising our children with me or I will do it alone, in which case, you will never see them again." My friend, the now-sixty-five-year-old daughter of this woman, smiles. She is proud of her mother. "He came home," she says.

Of the people who sit it out with honor, who wait for their spouses to "get over" extramarital infatuation, who martyr themselves for the cause of marriage, family or economics, I would want to know—was it worth it?

I have an eighty-year-old friend who tells me, "The hardest time in my life was when my husband had a love affair, and it lasted many years." I ask her, "Why didn't you leave?" revealing myself to be a member of the "me" generation, ill-equipped to handle frustration or psychic pain for more than a week, let alone years. "Oh, I thought of being passionate, of walking out the door," she replies, "but I had to think of the welfare of the family as a whole."

As I look at her family as a whole—the grandchildren, the companionship of husband and wife over the dinner table —I am almost persuaded. But then I don't know the price she paid: conceiving, bearing and raising his children, knowing all the while that his heart and passions were elsewhere. If these weren't intensely private matters, I would ask her, How long did it take for warmth to return to your body? To your heart?

In spite of a recent *Playboy* survey, which would have it that infidelity is a matter of fact of life—48 percent of men and 38 percent of women questioned said they were or had been engaged in extramarital affairs—infidelity is no fair. Somebody is left out. Somebody else is having all the fun. And even that isn't quite true, because guilt hovers about the door of the most carefree transgression. If you're very lucky, it won't knock louder than your heart or knees when you are in that illicit embrace.

It is that embrace that is visualized by anyone who has ever been betrayed: one's beloved in the arms and bed of another. Imagine it and tell me that your heart doesn't go belly-up like a dead fish.

Some of us struggled to understand the hippies' generosity of spirit. If they were willing to share spouses and lovers, we asked, why weren't we? After all, we had so much in common: make love not war—we agreed there; eat grains not flesh—sound nutrition. We thought that our desire for fidelity must be small and selfish, some tight little knot in our hearts, a wasting disease of our souls.

Now, I wonder. How much did the flower children really know about love? In infidelity someone is the outsider. Being an outsider hurts. Memories of birthday parties we weren't invited to, teams we weren't chosen for, being a child in a world run by and for grown-ups. Betrayal dredges up all these old feelings, raw and fresh as if age had neglected to install a protective layer of insulation between childhood and adulthood.

So I question the honorable selflessness of Henry James's Maggie, who desires not only the return of her husband but that he be protected from guilt and loss of honor. I question the hippies' magnanimous gestures. I question those who said of their "unsuspecting" spouses, "He [or she] will never find out." "It had nothing to do with you." That's like a pickpocket leaving behind a note saying, "Nothing personal." It may not be personal, but all the same you've been robbed. You've been had.

In *The Golden Bowl* and *The Good Soldier,* hearts and circumstances failed to mesh. The prince married Maggie because he couldn't afford to marry his true but penniless love. Obligations of their parents bound Leonora and Edward. In the enlightened 1980s it is hoped that we marry for love.

A friend of mine, divorced for ten sexually active years before remarriage, tells me: "I never knew that fidelity could feel so good. There is something lush about each encounter when you both know that each of you is the only one."

I would describe it as a feeling of being alone in the world without loneliness. Of being complete but uncrowded. Of peace and security. Like finding yourself under a tropical sun in February, or listening to Stern and Rose play Brahms's "Double Concerto." Or having your newborn, still connected by a cord, stare straight into your eyes. Nothing to give up without a gun.

What Happened
to Cynthia Koestler?

In his essay "Three Good Women," Montaigne writes of women who committed suicide with their husbands. Only in the case of Paulina, wife of Seneca, did the attempt fail. But, says Montaigne, such failure did not diminish her honor, virtue and devotion, "showing by the pallor of her face how much of life had flowed away through her wounds."

He tells of Pliny the Younger's neighbor, who suffered from an incurable disease and whose wife persuaded him to leap with her from their window into the sea. She promised that he would die in her arms. "But for fear that the closeness of her embrace might be loosened by the fall and by terror, she had herself tightly bound and attached to him around the waist."

And Arria, who took her life to encourage her husband, Paetus, to do likewise after his imprisonment by the Emperor Claudius. Plunging her husband's dagger into her breast and then placing the bloodied weapon into his hand, she exhorted him, "Believe me, the wound that I have made does not pain me, but the wound that you are to give yourself, that O Paetus, pains me."

Was this the pain that led Cynthia Koestler to join her husband in mutual suicide? There is no telling. No Roman historian was standing by in 1983 to bring us the final story. We know that writer Arthur Koestler, seventy-seven years old, was suffering from leukemia and Parkinson's disease but that his wife, some twenty years his junior, "was not known to have had any grave ailment." A broken heart does not qualify as a grave ailment. Their close friend Melvin Lasky tells us that "their marriage was almost impossibly close; her devotion to him was like no other wife's I have ever known."

I fear for "devoted" wives. I refuse to idealize these women and their endings. I cannot see death as the proper outcome of a good marriage, nor can I hold self-sacrifice as a standard of devotion. I am sorry, Montaigne, but I cannot agree that to qualify for "goodness" I must tie myself to the waist of another in the plunge for death or life. I understand that loving is giving of the self. I will not be persuaded that that includes giving up the self.

Of "impossible closeness" I would say, Beware. When two hearts beat as one, one of those hearts is in hiding.

A man in the business of finding hearts, a specialized detective of sorts, a psychoanalyst, described the process of analysis as "the longest goodbye." I would describe all loving as the longest goodbye. Starting with our parents, who taught us of gravity and our own perimeters, who painted the world of experience in the vibrant finger paints of words. "Me," "you," "exciting," "fun," "happy," "sad,"—real feelings in a real world painted in primary colors and illuminated by a spotlight. We were given a self and bade goodbye.

And in our adult lives the passion of our couplings comes in part from the knowledge that we are close, we are bound, we merge and say goodbye.

Every morning as we part for work or wave a child off to school, we are murmuring small *adieux,* often without a twinge of the heart. This is practice built into the system, preparation for what is to come—the final and most fearsome of farewells.

Some fear the final farewell so completely that they refuse to live as separate individuals, to practice their goodbyes. They refuse to take part in the drill, to march up and down the heart's cutting edge. So frightened are they of separation that they attempt to blend their own boundaries with those of their beloved. They believe that by moving side by side they will become one. That eventually, like the tigers in "Little Black Sambo," their frenzied attachment will melt them down into a common ghee.

And there are those who will not enter into intense relationships, will not open themselves to another, who are afraid of intimacy because "it will hurt too much when it ends." They say goodbye before they have ever said hello.

The best marriages I know are between people whose greetings are joyous and farewells sad, whose individuality is cherished and encouraged. Their mergings are limited to their lovemaking, to which they bring fearless, eager and vulnerable selves. Afterward they dust off the sharp edges of their lines of demarcation and go about their lives.

They are like the crowds that gather on beaches and mountaintops to watch the sunset. They act as if they don't know how this show ends. They approach with wonder. Their quiet comments can be heard as darkened sky gives way to rose, to violet, to yellow. But then there is silence and stillness when the show ends, when night has finally and irrevocably swallowed day. The curtain has come down, but the audience remains for one moment of numbed disbelief. Then they stand up, straighten their skirts, adjust their ties and move out into darkness.

Just more practice. We keep coming to the sunsets to remind ourselves that there will never be another quite like it, to feel the ache and to relearn that grief eventually spreads out against the sky, softens and dissipates.

What happened, Cynthia Koestler? How did you forget

this? Or did you never practice? Did you truly believe that you would be left forever in gloom when the brilliance of your husband's light flickered and was snuffed out? Did your disease feel as fatal as his actually was? At what point are we so bound in life that death for one must mean death for the other? Even orchids, attached as they are to trees, flesh to bark, pollen to sap, continue to bloom after their tree is rootless and dry.

I grieve for you, Mrs. Koestler. I think that upon autopsy it might be revealed that there are recesses of our hearts that match. I too have dreamed of lassoing the sun, of digging in my heels so that spurs kick up the dust as I am dragged over the horizon. I too feel the draw of Pliny's neighbors' mutual plunge. The idea of final merging, of being bound waist to waist, is not without its appeal. Mine is also a powerful love. But somehow I see it differently.

I don't know where the medical examiner would find that the paths of our hearts changed course. Have I built a wall where yours is a sluice? Am I brook where you are slough? There's no telling.

But I must part company with Paulina, with Arria. I will not have my virtue rest on self-inflicted wounds. And I must part company with you, Mrs. Koestler, because I will not surrender myself in silence or in screams. I will take the plunge for life. But lest my resolve "be loosened by terror," I will bind myself about the waist with a fierce and stubborn knot and attach it to my own heart.

Hera and
the Workplace

When Hera sent a gadfly to chase Io out of Greece into Egypt, when she ordered all lands to refuse shelter to the pregnant Leto, and arranged for Semele to be burned alive, it wasn't because her husband, Zeus, was taking business trips with these comely associates. Circumstances have changed but Hera's legacy lives on.

Out of the new enlightenment, out of the feminist movement, out of the thrust for equality for women in the workplace is born a whole new generation of Heras. "She is my 'sister,' " a friend says of the attractive associate with whom her husband spends his workdays, travels on business and meets the crisis of deadlines as a comrade in arms. "She is the one we all worked to bring along, she is living up to the feminist ideal. And I resent and fear her."

Understandable. Who among us is sanguine about these situations? But the times and our own ideals insist that we must be. Insist that we ignore the heart that cringes and twists and contorts with jealousy. Dryden's "jaundice of the soul." After all, we are mature women. We are no longer the dependent child-wives. We are the women working with other women's husbands. We are both cause and effect. We are the new jealous.

In the past, jealousies arising out of the work situation were largely muted by the fact that the presence of women was limited to "lowly" office assistants. Past generations of wives, blatantly sexist and unburdened by any sense of sisterhood, simply assumed that these women were not suitable "wife material" and therefore not serious threats. A man might dally with his secretary, but his corporation and his ambition would discourage his making an "honest woman" of her. The little woman back home had been carefully groomed for her important role as corporate wife. Prejudice, the threat of scandal and small minds protected her.

No more. Wives have met their match in the women who work with their husbands. These women have the strength necessary to have found their niche in the male world. They are intelligent and accomplished. Whether or not they are physically attractive is irrelevant since their attraction comes from the intimacy of sharing the same work.

There is a camaraderie, a closeness. They are buddies. They speak the same language, share office politics and meals. She really cares that a company is threatening to take over their client. She understands factoring and arbitrage and municipal bonds. When he talks about the day's strangulated hernia or coronary bypass, her eyes don't glaze over. She questions the procedure and suggests improvements in technique.

She is, in other words, ideal. Jealousy does that. It exaggerates our own shortcomings and the other's perfections. Jealousy makes no sense. It makes us scorn the one we idealize. It makes us infantile when we need to be mature. It makes us insane when a cool head is called for. It makes us guilty because the fantasies of harm we wish upon the object of our jealousy, if realized, could send us up for fifty years to life.

Oh yes, Hera is alive and well in the heart of the jealous

spouse of either sex. Show me a husband who is indifferent to the number of hours spent or miles covered by his wife in the company of a male colleague and I will show you a stone. If he breathes, he worries. If he worries, he joins the rest of us out there on the lunatic fringe.

On an airless, ninety degree, New York City morning as I was about to depart for my law firm's summer outing at a country club, my husband asked if there would be swimming. I replied that I certainly hoped so. "You mean that you will wear a bathing suit?" The look of alarm softened my desire for the obvious sarcastic response. We had left the realm of reason. It was highly unlikely that as I approached the diving board, old Monroe film clips would start running through the minds of my colleagues. It would not be imagined that a calendar girl had stepped from print to flesh, from gas station wall to Piping Rock poolside. No dazed, love-struck mass of Wall Street attorneys was going to dive in after me for a closer look, a touch, an underwater embrace. None, that is, except those parading through my husband's mind's eye—jealousy's functioning eye.

Was I honored by this exaggeration of my sex appeal? No. Did I respond with sympathy for his imagined plight? Again, no. Jealousy sabotages one's more understanding self. As a lawyer, I immediately thought of it in terms of rights. What right did he have to think such things?

No right. But jealousy has nothing to do with rights. Jealousy is a freak of nature. Along with sharks and cockroaches, it should have become extinct. Its only purpose is to inspire great literature. Without it we would not have *Othello* or *Medea* or some fine lines from *Paradise Lost.*

Jealousy does not protect love. It does not bind the family of man, guard the balance of power or ecosystems. It does not serve as an aid to navigation for heart or eye. It blinds, it warps, it distorts.

If it were a bacterial antigen, the Centers for Disease Control in Atlanta would have brilliant researchers on a

round-the-clock search for an antibody. There would be
boxes for coin contributions at cashiers' counters in restaurants. If it were a crop-destroying pest, the ban on DDT
would be lifted. If it were standing in the way of high finance
and industry, it would be threatened with warfare. But it is a
matter of the heart and those matters have always been rele-
gated to the realm of private agony and less private art.

Given all this, how to protect the self and one's beloved
from its destruction? I would start with corporations.
Granted, they are not known for alert sensitivity; but if the
exclusivity of the work situation is causing pain, then they
should open their social affairs to spouses. I know the reason
given for not encouraging wives of ballplayers to accompany
their husbands on the road, but I doubt that the team spirit of
law firms, hospitals, corporations or banks will suffer in the
face of "outsiders." Surely the parties won't be duller.

For our own parts, I suppose we could invite them
around . . . these objects of our jealousy, these perfect
women, large of chest and slim of ankle, multiply orgasmic
and mentally astute. In jealousy, what you don't see does hurt
you. Expose the imagined ideals to the light and your mind's
eye will squint.

I suppose that we should learn to respond to this Hera-
dic madness with generosity of spirit. When a friend of mine
remarked to her husband that his female associate "certainly
isn't very attractive," he should not have responded, "Yes,
she is." We could be kind when we are defensive. I could
have made one mad but ultimately wise gesture that hot and
crazy day long ago and put my bathing suit in my husband's
briefcase for safekeeping. For the safekeeping of his otherwise perfect sanity.

Unrequited Love

Does the imagination dwell the most
upon a woman won or woman lost?
(W. B. YEATS, "The Tower")

"There's nothing worse than unrequited love," I tell my daughter in an attempt to soothe with sweet empathy.

"Yes, there is," she replies. "Rejection."

Well, yes and no. Rejection is a quick jab to the heart, while unrequited love is a prolonged stranglehold. Rejection leaves you alone on the street corner knowing exactly where you stand. Unrequited love leaves you staring wistfully up at his windows, hope and pain your constant companions.

Her horoscope for today reads, "Should anyone light a match near you, you will burn up in the flames of passion." I think it's probably true. But there's a difference between the unrequited loves of one's youth and those of later years. The youthful passions are as volatile as her stars and planets portend, but the difference is that the love is meant to remain unrequited. Should it suddenly requite, I am quite certain that fear and flight would replace fantasy and longing, even though the desire for the fulfillment of the dream is all consuming.

What is crueler to the heart than not being able to possess the object of its longing? It's positively un-American. We're supposed to be able to go out and get anything we set our minds to. Hard work, we are told, is all it takes. Geraldine Ferraro said it. So did Horatio Alger in his way. We believe in this. But the heart does not always obey.

What if the one desired is happily married to another? What if the object of adoration is our psychiatrist or school teacher or priest? What if we're simply not to his or her liking? Except for the hopelessness of the latter situation, the rules of restraint governing the others have been broken just often enough to shed a faint ray of hope along the way. Enough times to fuel our fantasies.

Literature, legend and the history of the world encourage us. Look at the fairy tales. Few happily-ever-after love stories are based on likely matches. The hero and heroine must see their way to truth through cinders and frog skins. It's the impossibility of reconciliation, union and bliss that keeps us reading to the end and cheering when the prince marries the peasant, the princess a frog. These stories set up an archetype of a beloved just beyond reach. There are those who will feel constrained to tell you that this is all based on incest taboos. That we are agitated by the unattainable because of our primal longings to challenge the Oedipal myth. Perhaps. But tell that to anyone who's pining for love and expect a cold shoulder for your trouble.

The pain is not without its pleasures. Petrarch knew it as did the hundreds of his love-sick translators and disciples.

> E bramo di perir, e cheggio aita;
> ed ho in odio me stesso, ed amo altrui:
> Pascomi di dolor; piangendo ride;
> Equ alemte mi spiace morte e vita.
> In questo state son, Donna, per vui.

(I cling to life, and yet would gladly perish;
Detest myself, and yet another cherish;
Feed upon grief; from grief my laughter borrow;
Death is a spear and life a poisoned arrow,
And in delight my fears take root and flourish.)[1]

The fourteenth-century "I freeze and yet I burn" school
of poets idealized women who were monotonously "cruel"
in their "virtue." Physical love existed only to provide meta-
phor, and although racked by desire, what the victim admired most in his tormentor was her chastity. The lady was
not for seduction, not even by variable caesura.

But stop! Earlier centuries' infatuation with love is to be
mocked by the "cool" generation, those of us whose hearts
were wounded in the sixties and hardened over with smooth,
numb, unyielding scar tissue. "I don't understand," an English professor scolded our college class in Renaissance poetry. "Why are you so frightened to love?" She compared us
unfavorably with Spenser, Sir Thomas Wyatt and Henry
Howard, Earl of Surrey. "So you declare your love and the
person doesn't love you back. So what?"

She was right to be concerned. She indicted us as emotional cowards and we were, in fact, guilty. None of us
wanted to repeat the pain. Repeated from what moments in
our history? We would have been hard pressed to tell. But we
all seemed to agree that it was better to have never loved at
all than to have loved and lost. We were "cool" all right, and
determined to keep a distance between the deliberations of
our minds and the beats of our hearts, to shut off imagination
lest it dwell on those we had lost.

Which is not to say that we didn't act out and act up. We
took on public rather than private passions. We marched on
Washington, we marched down Main Street, we "sat in" any

---

1. From Petrarch's "During the Life of Laura," Sonnet CIV, *The Sonnets of Petrarch.*
Translated by Joseph Auslander. Longmans, Green & Co., London, 1931.

place that had bad politics and a place to perch. We wrote petitions and position papers in place of love poems. It was easier for us to confront the heinous crimes of undeclared war and racial discrimination than our own bruised emotions. "I am a rock, I am an island. And a rock feels no pain and an island never cries," were lyrics of one of our favorite songs.

What is particularly suitable about unrequited love is that the love object remains ideal. If falling 'in love is an idealization of the other, then loving is an acceptance that the ideal creature gives way, with time, to one who is flawed, but lovable nonetheless. One never gets close enough to the unrequited love object to see him or her before morning coffee or after a week of flu. The breakfast table, the bridal chamber are dreamed of, but their realities never confronted. Removed from view are the irrationalities, irascibilities, hurt feelings, grumps, grunts and groans of real people in real gardens. The one who will never be ours will never be subjected to our scrutiny. His perfections will glow from the distance like a lighthouse on which we can stay our sights.

Perhaps this is why people fall in love with movie stars and celebrities. These are not people leaving footsteps in our lives. We can allow ourselves the luxury of believing in their perfection, knowing that it will never be tested. One loved from afar will never disappoint us with bad table manners or a propensity for sulking.

"He's perfect" is the expression I hear from teenage girls when they are in love with someone unavailable. And who can blame them for wanting to believe it? No matter how savvy we are, we never seem to tire of the idea that the human being is perfectable and if we ourselves have failed, there must be someone out there who has succeeded, to whom we can attach ourselves and soak up the glory.

Perhaps in the sixties we were unwilling to set our hearts loose like Frisbees because it wasn't safe out there. It became increasingly apparent that the dream of world peace, a stubborn holdover from "the war to end all wars," was a factual impossibility. Television brought that home to us every night. Too much aggression and violence, too many wars being fought in too many places to ever be brought under control. Any notion that we, baby-boom children conceived out of optimism, were cherished was quickly dispelled by our numbers being decreased in Vietnam, at Kent State, in Mississippi. We as a group did not have enough time for idealization, to revel in it, be disappointed by some small human flaw, and move on to find the next ideal. We came to believe that if we wore our hearts on our sleeves they would be shot off.

Our earlier days had been spent growing up in country communities, small towns and slick new suburbs that still held their promise. Kids had not started committing suicide casually, giving beer parties and trashing their homes or making dope connections at school. We had a steady diet of Howdy Doody and Kate Smith. Television sold us goodness and hopefulness as if they were surprises inside a box of Cracker Jacks. We were too young to notice the Korean War, but just old enough to absorb the romance of the time. Movie magazines, Elizabeth Taylor's lavender eyes, *Seven Brides for Seven Brothers.*

In adolescence, we were ripe to fall in love with the urbane, movie star-handsome young senator from Massachusetts who was elected President. We who believed in heroes had a live one. When we were seventeen he was assassinated.

I don't think that my generation is still recovering. I think that my generation has given up the hope of recovery. Like brutalized children who take to the streets to live by fists and wits, we have adopted lives remote from feeling. There are two defenses to too much pain: an identification with the aggressor or a retreat into numbness. Aaron Spelling, television producer of popular nighttime soaps, is getting rich on his understanding of the latter. He knows that this generation wants to be served programming as bland and satisfying as a peanut butter and marshmallow fluff sandwich; he understands the appeal of the simplistic world of Howdy Doody in which the good guy is always good (Howdy), the villain on the verge of redemption (Mr. Bluster) and the woman forever beautiful (Princess Summerfall Winterspring). He knows his viewers will turn off their sets if confronted with issues that open wounds inflicted when they stepped away from television and into an adolescence beseiged by unchecked violence.

Risks with the heart are not to be taken. Imagination must not have its way. We've pined long enough. When Petrarch lamented unattainable love, he could do so with gusto because there was a beginning, middle and end to heartache as structured by the poem. But our pain has failed to find a structure that would allow the heart to come out of hiding. We move through your midst as ordinary civilians but feel akin to the soldiers who make the news every once in a while when they emerge, hands raised in surrender, from Pacific islands where they've hidden for forty years, not knowing that World War II is over.

That war and "our" wars—Vietnam, the civil rights movement—did not touch my daughter's generation. John Kennedy, Andrew Goodman, Martin Luther King, the soldier in Vietnam are history to her, and being history, they can neither belong to nor harm her. Their demise has not left blood and tears on her coat sleeve.

There is nothing worse than unrequited love, I, a sixties' child, tell my daughter, and she, whose heart is swollen with it, tells me, "Yes, there is." She dares stand near flame in spite of her horoscope. For her, heartache is not something to be avoided at all costs. There can be a romance to it. It can be welcomed and savored, Petrarch style. It can make one feel alive.

There's No Accounting for Love

CLINTON, TENN., MARCH 7 (UPI)—"Mary Evans, a lawyer who fell so deeply in love with the killer she was defending that she helped him escape, pleaded guilty today . . . Her lawyer said she would enter a mental hospital."

Maybe we should join her there. I think that the only difference between Mary Evans and the rest of us is that we weren't hauled before the judge as a result of falling in love.

Her case raises some interesting questions. According to Freud, we fall in love with the person who is as similar to the parent of the opposite sex (here comes the important part) as we can stand. Some of us can stand more than others. Mary Evans makes us wonder.

Now, I don't know anything about her dad. Maybe he had a criminal streak. On the other hand, maybe he's on the board of overseers of Brushy Mountain State Penitentiary, from which his daughter's client escaped. I don't know. But I do know about some other couplings that UPI and the courts failed to pick up.

My friend Alice is a violinist in a symphony orchestra. Her mother-in-law plays the bassoon. Alice's husband is a talented but unemployed musician whom she supports, just as her mother had supported her father.

I have another friend who thought she had made a clean break. Her father is a banker whose father was a banker before him. His clubs admit members exclusively like himself. Old money, WASP lineage, cool emotions kept strictly under control. My friend lives in a loft in the Bowery with a black sculptor formerly active in SDS. There's just one hitch. He has the same name and is the same age as Dad. It's embarrassing to be caught out in the psychological cold, id exposed. A bit like those dreams in which you remember to show up for the party but forget to wear clothes.

You could ask a psychiatrist, "Why would a woman whose business is the law fall in love with a criminal?" and you might get a pretty good answer. You could ask Mary Evans' fellow workers and chances are they'll look surprised and say, "She was a real nice girl." Someone always does. They'll speak of happier times and show you photographs of her dressed in tailored suits and low-heeled pumps.

But these aren't the answers I'm interested in. I want to know why anybody falls in love with anybody.

Pick a random group of couples on a bus, in a resort, on the street and you'll have to admit that the pairings are about as bizarre as the lawyer and the murderer. Sweet, docile men appearing apologetic in the company of huge, bellowing women. George Price cartoons. Regal women with street kid husbands. Party lovers with recluses. Bill Buckley types with mates who say "irregardless." There's no accounting for it.

I approached a source, a woman still in love (madly) with her husband of seventeen years. "What makes you feel this way?" I asked. She looked surprised, then thought quietly for about half a minute and answered, "I think it's his bones. There's something about his bony elbows and knees." Well, all right. She looked helpless. I changed the subject.

It may not lead us to a life of crime, but love usually catches us off guard. I'm not talking about those couples who are together for convenience, money or because, like being in Philadelphia, it's better than the alternative. I'm talking about those whose lawyers would plead, "not guilty by reason of insanity."

What are the legal elements needed to make such a defense? The McNaughton Rule won't suffice. That rule asks, did the defendant know the difference between right and wrong? Did he suffer from a mental defect which at the time made it impossible for him to understand the wrongfulness of his acts? No, that won't do. Perhaps a rush-of-blood test? A shaking knees test? Unlikely. Perhaps a Todd-Dickinson test. Consider the state described by poet Emily Dickinson's brother, the august Austin Dickinson, in a letter to his mistress, the married Mabel Loomis Todd. "My whole being craved you, so I could hardly control the action of my mind."

Mabel Loomis Todd and Austin Dickinson didn't face prison, but they did face a nineteenth-century New England community's attitude toward adultery. And yet they persisted with their passionate affair. Perhaps precisely because of that community. Only through the madness of falling in love could they be free of its hold. Only in an apparent loss of control could they gain control of their own lives. Free of small-town mores, they claimed their destinies.

Maybe that was Mary Evan's motivation. In the 1980s everything is susceptible, if not to one's neighbor's, then surely to science's probing and expository. "Did you know," an excited scientist explains to me, "that we learn more about the brain every day than we have known over the past hundred years?" Poor brain, its privacy once inviolate within a bony, secret-keeping skull now tapped for revelation.

But in love we are beyond reason and scientific probes. It is in this state of madness that we enter the mysteries. Hook Mabel Loomis Todd or Mary Evans up to a brain scan, take blood samples, monitor their sleep and you're not going to find a thing.

A few years ago, noted psychoanalyst Charles Fisher,

M.D., presented colleagues with the results of his research into sleep and sexuality. For an hour the lecture was heavy with the importance of dream state, pulse and heart rate, vaginal tumescence and temperature change, rapid eye movement and the size and frequency of penal erection. Then there was a moment of silence. Fisher put down his papers, looked out at his gray-beard audience and shrugged. "So now we know she dreams. But does she dream of me?"

Mary Evans isn't about to tell. There is autonomy in being beyond reason, especially if you can do it and stay out of jail.

The Obdurate Attender

Many of us have known the Person Who Wouldn't Go Away, whether it was a persistent boy in eighth grade, a nostalgic old flame or just a guy who took a liking to us and liked and liked and liked beyond all reason. And those of us raised never to hurt feelings or step on toes suffered a strange, almost benevolent torture. We became the victims of someone else's determined heart.

"Christopher made the card himself," the sniffling voice reports over the line from Austin to New York. My friend tells me that it is a gloomy, rainy day, that one of her kids just knocked out another's tooth with a soccer ball, that her four-year-old daughter is walking around the house carrying the cat by its ears and has made a brief detour to empty a box of staples into her unsuspecting brother's glass of milk. "He was my boyfriend when I was sixteen, and suddenly this card came today."

She begins to wail: "I thought that someday I would be a different person, that I would forget him. That I wouldn't care anymore." But he has insinuated himself back into her life more than twenty years later and two thousand miles from their original home. With a hand-drawn picture of a Coca-Cola bottle (it had been their favorite drink) and the words, "You're the real thing," he has filled her with wistful thoughts—the torment of a rainy day when one is forty and susceptible to musings on what might have been. A friendly but foreboding intrusion into an otherwise settled life.

When I was in eighth grade a classmate used to leave notes on my desk. Because writing was something he had never been able to master, even after three years in eighth grade, his messages were blocked out with the careful anonymity of ransom notes, and they filled me with almost as much dread. Why? What was so frightening about a smudged piece of paper bearing my name?

The words were far from menacing. In fact, they were bland if not flattering. "You are nice" or "I like your hair." So why the vague sense of terror? Because I was too young to understand that it had nothing to do with me, that obsessions are not to be taken personally.

It's unsettling to have another's unwanted passions invade your life. It's like a bird crashing into a window by your side while you are looking the other way and thinking that all is right with the world. Suddenly there is a wounded bird at your feet. Now what? Put on rubber gloves, pick it up and drive ninety miles an hour to the ASPCA? Wait for it to die and then bury it? Walk away?

I have a friend who tried the walking-away method and the bird kept resurrecting itself and pecking at her shoulders, her neck, her hair. "This was a man who saw me as the answer to his prayers. He had a gloss of courtliness and generosity but was basically evil." She explains: "He insisted on sending flowers to me at home. Dozens of roses. I kept telling him that it was very awkward. What were my husband and children to think? He persisted." She was finally driven to a solution that she now describes as "some kind of bizarre identification with the oppressor." To dispose of the flowers she would put them in a shopping bag, drive to a poor part of

town, look for a clothesline that was weighted to the ground
with diapers, men's work clothes; if they were tattered, so
much the better. She would sneak up to the door and leave
the flowers on the doorstep. She says that she made "beautiful cards and signed them, 'From someone who admires this
family.' "

She also found a nursing home where she could sit in the
lobby and learn the names of the residents. She would have
the flowers delivered to them on a rotating basis with cards
that read, "To Mrs. Miller from someone who thinks you're
swell." Or "To Fran Murray from someone who thinks you
have beautiful eyes."

But she tired of these adventures and was enraged that
her pursuer was driving her to such madness. She finally told
him that if he did not go away she would send her husband to
deal with him personally. "But to this day, eighteen years
later, I sometimes get a card or small gift. If I'm lucky, it only
ruins my day. If I'm not, it ruins my week."

Basically, what she describes is a terrible invasion of privacy. As life proceeds along, one gathers friends, commit-
ments, roots, cares, and suddenly, unconnected to all of this
comes a demand, "Remember ME!"

Common-law battery was defined as "an unwanted
touching." Unwanted touchings have included subway fond-
lings and the kiss from the woman who saw you on the street
and mistook you, a stranger, for her aunt Gladys. But what to
do about unwanted touchings of your life? The chocolates
delivered to your door like Snow White's apple?

Take John Hinckley, for instance. There was nothing
Jody Foster could do to inure herself or dissuade him. Only
an arrest on an assassination attempt has kept him from camp-
ing outside her door.

There ought to be a way that my friend with the flowers
could send her old suitor's unwanted correspondence back
on a stream of flame that would land at his feet, fizzle and
then play a recorded message, something along the line of a

singing telegram: "No way, Jose!" or "Get back, Jack!" or "Get on the bus, Gus!"

The worst part is that one feels victimized, helpless before these unwanted attentions. One friend finally had to retreat behind her husband's strength: another hopes to become a different person. I waited, waited for the end of eighth grade when I would be safely ensconced in an all girls' boarding school.

Of course the obdurate attender is not always male. Madness and passion will have their way regardless of the psyche's gender. In his movie *The Story of Adele H.,* François Truffaut retraced the obsessed journey of Victor Hugo's younger daughter from Guernsey to Halifax to the West Indies in pursuit of the indifferent Lieutenant Pinson.

And so it goes, from man to woman, from woman to man—a passionate but actually impersonal obsession, a piece of fiction. A fantasy fed on the hot blood of a blind heart.

Even if you shake the obsessed until his teeth knock, even if you dunk his head in cold water, even if you spell out your faults, he will insist that you are ideal. Even if you say, "You mean nothing to me," he will respond, "You don't know your own heart." Maybe your eyes are like his mother's, the way you cross your legs reminds him of the babysitter he had when he was three, you're a first grade teacher and that was his first love. At any rate, it has nothing to do with you.

What to do? I don't know. I'm the person who still remembers the eighth-grade pursuer. I think the solution might lie somewhere along the lines of a friend's response to what she finds a minor but irritating intrusion. When a stranger says, "Have a nice day," she responds: "No thank you. I have other plans."

The Bag Lady

Whenever I see a bag lady, I see myself slipping past the edge of time and space into an abandoned doorway. "We are all bag ladies in our souls," says a friend who has certainly had her share of successes. She tells me of riding a bus recently when a bag lady climbed on, heaving herself and her possessions through the door and up the steps. Some sense of pride or purpose or both pushed her past the seats reserved for the handicapped and elderly, down the aisle to the back where one long, overheated seat served as an inspection table for the contents of her bags.

The men continued to read their papers. "But the women became very tense, as if she were sending a current through them," my friend recounted. They sat up straighter, drew their knees together and clutched at whatever was on their laps. When she got up to leave, there wasn't a woman on that bus who didn't turn to watch her safely down the steps, and gaze after her until she was no longer in sight. She left behind a scent of vulnerability.

It is a fearful scent of our own. Not Proust's madeleines, but it sets off our imaginings. We can see ourselves rummag-

ing through trash cans, searching for a tin can because it will
make a perfect cup, rejoicing in rags because they warm the
feet. Even women with regular jobs can imagine this. Even
those with five-piece place settings for twelve.

The other day as I was walking up Third Avenue, I was
startled by the rushed breath of a cough sweeping my ankle.
It came from a mouth set among rags, sucking the last smoke
from a used cigarette. Her head was propped against the
doorway, her feet within inches of a man who stood reading
the menu in a restaurant's window. If she had had a sense of
whimsy, she could have stuck her bare, nailless toe into the
cuff of his pinstripe pants. His nostrils flared for a moment,
took in the smell but failed to identify it as urine mixed with
four layers of clothing mixed with twice-eaten food mixed
with oozing sores.

We know that, like meteors, all that keeps us in orbit and
shining—away from that doorway, those garbage piles—is
our faith in gravity. In choosing love as the star to which we
attach the heart's invisible threads, we shoot through the atmosphere, cling as we spin through the galaxy and hold on
for dear life because we know that stars have quirks. Why,
just the other day one that had lost its grip fell through the
roof of a house in Wethersfield, Conn.

I've known other stars to fall into black holes in space.
Sucked in, crushed and extinguished. Of course there was no
escape. Nothing ever gets out of a black hole. And there is
no help for it. No cosmologist can go in with forceps and
yank out a star.

So we dig our toes into earth for a gritty hold. We collect
antiques and achievements to plant ourselves in place. But we
fall for love, we hope for eternity, and we see the evanes-
cence of things, knowing that where we wish for monuments
there are only mists.

If all goes well, our children grow up and leave us. According to national statistics, the men we love will predecease
us or suddenly find commitment not to their liking. The

more we open our hearts, which seems to be the way with
women, the more vulnerable we are if cast adrift. What we
gather about us can be carried in bags. What we hold dear is
easily mobilized.

No job can stay us. No wealth can shield us from the
fear that someday we will be left alone, shot forth from our
magnetic field. We see our hearts bend with the burden of
bags, move with rhythm but without purpose, gather in the
castoffs of strangers' lives because we have lost faith in our
own.

Is this why Helen Frankenthaler stains color into oversized canvas? Why Judith Jamison perfects her leaps? Why
Rosalyn Tureck spins and spins and spins Bach fugues,
preludes and fantasies? To weave herself into the fabric of his
immortality? Is this why Lady Bird Johnson roots herself to
the earth with wildflowers, and the astronaut Dr. Sally K.
Ride offers herself up to space? Is this why I went to law
school?

Perhaps.

Certainly centuries of legal principle should hold me in
place. And certainly my heart would come to rest in an office
with a river view and a secretary outside the door.

"Making it," "having it all," securing our futures have
been motivated in no small way by our identification with the
bag lady. Our accomplishments, titles and pension plans were
to protect us from the future we saw out of the corners of our
eyes as we stalked the streets or rode the buses.

But in crowded theaters and on quiet walks we whisper
of our fears. "We are held in place by wrapped rags and
shopping carts."

When I decided to leave the practice of law, a concerned
and careerless friend with grown children and an over-
worked husband called to register her distress: "If you become too involved with your husband and children there will
be nothing left of you in the end. What about your auton-

omy?'' She might as well have asked, ''What about the bag lady?'' We both knew that was what she meant.

I did not tell her that neither oil and gas deals nor victories in the New York Court of Appeals banished the woman hovering above me like a Chagall clock. Walking home late at night with a heavy briefcase in my hand, I had often fallen into step with a bag lady pushing her cart. I felt that I was walking with my future.

I understand my friend's concern. She assumed, as many of us have, that careers guarantee an end to dependency and vulnerability. She forgot that these are matters of the heart that shy away from reason's persistent grasp. They are the consequence of need, caring, kindness, generosity and tenderness—those things which are a woman's soul first and last, no matter how much power and prestige are pressed on top.

On Madison Avenue between Seventy-fifth and Eighty-eighth Streets you can see a bag lady who travels with a cat. How she lassoed it and why it complied is a mystery. But I can guess why she captured and tethered it to her cart. That cat sits on top of her trash as its crowning glory, the ultimate find—a beating heart.

I imagine that in her dreams she forgets which is the self and which is the cat. He gives her a vision of herself as sleek and bound in fur. She gives him her scraps. Outside the restaurant they eat fettuccine Alfredo caught in discarded mussel shells.

Such is love.

If the Child Is Father of the Man, Then Who Am I and Who Is She?

Bonding

Animals and Eskimos bite off the umbilical cord. In the confusion and decorum of our delivery rooms, one is rarely certain when it was done or how. The only evidence is a flushed flower of a wound in the middle of a protruding belly. "X" marks the spot. Do they expect us to believe that? Much better to have the aftertaste of severance in the mouth. To remind us and make it certain.

There is a primitive plain, something like the dark side of the moon, on which we merge with our children. Through this tenebrous gloom, we can hardly decipher them as separate souls with passions rising from their own sources.

This morning, after verbally lashing my daughter, I felt the resulting wound as if it were my own. Like those struggling-for-the-gun scenes in detective movies where the enemies grapple in the grass and roll in mud, each grabbing for the gun and leaving the viewer in suspense, whose flesh muffled the resulting explosion? Mine, I think. My body shakes with the imagined blow when in fact it was reverberation that rocked me. The hypothetical blood that flowed was not my own except where genes and typing made it so. It's hard to keep it straight.

I will search the wound of bitter argument as if I were a pathologist seeking cause and effect in tissue and bone.

Lately the focus of conscientious, upward-scale, new parents is "bonding." They touch their babies a lot. They read of the importance of interaction, approaching it with the formality of fifteenth-century courtship. I have a friend who included the family dog in the process, making it sleep in the baby's room for purposes of bonding. I think they've got it all wrong.

Bonding happens in spite of ourselves. It even happens in families where parents don't have degrees in anthropology or years of psychoanalysis under their belts. It was happening before it was given a name and prominent place in how-to-raise-your-children columns in women's magazines. It happens whether we are good or bad parents. A drowning victim reaches toward light, grabbing any lifeline thrown. Just try to unclench those tiny fingers.

Don't say we haven't been warned. The literature is full of fused females. Antoinette and Annette in Jean Rhys's *Wide Sargasso Sea*. Lily and Anna in Susanna Moore's *My Old Sweetheart*. Daughters in thrall to their mothers, mothers in thrall to themselves. Neither the mothers' respective insanities nor eventual deaths could sever these daughters and liberate them into a sense of where the self began and Mother left off. For Antoinette the result was a final fusing with her mother in madness. For Lily it was to give birth to a daughter, name her Anna after her mother and play out the scenes of an earlier life, changing the history of her childhood by being a mother different from her own. "I have made her [my daughter] my talisman: if she is happy, then I am not my mother."

My talisman is off to take her college entrance exams. You would think the tests were mine, so cold my hands, so wakeful my night. I'm not alone in forgetting who is going to college and who is staying home. Idealization and self-delusion are rampant among those of us who are parents of sixteen-year-olds. In the dream of what we want for ourselves we neglect the applicant's identity. It doesn't matter whether the kid's sentences are filled with sounds where words should be. It doesn't matter if exam scores are poor, they will be disregarded, "She doesn't test well." If grades are below par, a miraculous climb is envisioned, "As soon as she buckles down." As we sally forth visiting universities, we are as full of puffery and good intentions as Chaucer's pilgrims. We will tell you, if asked, why we "longen . . . to goon on pilgrimages," that it is what is best for the child. That is true to the same extent that the pilgrimage to Canterbury was motivated by religious fervor.

We trek off to colleges in a sort of dream state, our feet moved by what we have or have not accomplished in our own lives as much as our wishes for the lives of our children. It's a wonder admissions officers can work their way through these tortuous, psychological mazes. It's a wonder that any child does. After all, we are telling them that we are perfectly rational and know exactly what we're doing and they, taking us for adults, imbue us with a certain degree of credibility.

This fall, pilot whales beached themselves on Cape Cod. A watery Jonestown. Nobody knows why it happened. Mites in the ears? Scrambled radar? A virus? Some suggest geomagnetic anomalies or a primordial desire for terra firma. All we know for sure is that these creatures adept at celestial navigation answered a perverse call and lost their way. So it is when the boundaries between ourselves and our children blur. We are pulled by forces we don't understand. Primitive, pulsing, insistent.

When poetry failed, Hart Crane could only rid himself of his mother with a final suicidal plunge into the sea. It's not necessary to go that far to kill off parts of the self and the other in order to achieve a perfect fit. We can merely distort as one does when swimming under water with open eyes and no mask. A salty rush between the lids and what you have before you is a soft and gentle blending. Stinging spines of sea urchins become spongy shadows. Jagged fingers of flame coral perform a dance of gentle beckoning until they brush against a cold wet thigh and break the skin's surface green. Then we are shocked into remembering, then we begin a steady stroke toward shore.

Her tears this morning had the effect of that sharp shock. There is an aftertaste of their salt in my mouth. They were as startling as blood, springing from a source that is her mystery, from depths not meant for my plunge.

From beginning to end this is a wet and blood-smeared voyage, this begetting and birthing and moving away. Over and over we reenact it, take it from the top until we get it right, new versions of that original scene when our own dark and nourishing sea fell upon us from the body suspended by feet above where we lay. Our waters born by those Aquarius of our divining. Over and over again they emerge to remind us who they are. Until finally we plant teeth into sinew and bite, often in a fury to which they've driven us, to force us to open our mouths and attack. There is a rush in the ears, we know we are drowning but the gnashing continues until our teeth snap together. And we surface and survive. Surface and separate.

My Daughter
the Princess,
Her Mother the Queen

It's happened. She has seen us and found us wanting. I've been awaiting this event ever since she turned twelve, the age I was when I became disenchanted with my own parents. There we were, the four of us, mother, father, younger sister and I, stopping off at Zip's Diner, the shiniest edifice within a fifty-mile radius of this Connecticut farmland. It stood like a beacon, a glittering silver rectangle with a flashing red sign. Zip's! Zip's! Zip's! On and off, announcing itself in neon twenty-four hours a day. You could get a fine milkshake there, and a hamburger patted into shape by the cook's fat, chapped hands. The air was full of flying gristle and grease and the sweet aroma of hot, red meat.

But that day, instead of being eager to enter that box wrapped as brightly as a birthday gift, I was anguished. I would be revealed as a member of this family. I walked several steps behind the other three, hoping that the people within would not identify me as a member of this tribe. The waitress with hair the color of poached salmon and eyebrows penciled to match, the truck driver smelling of stale cigarette smoke and Juicy Fruit gum, the woman wearing pale blue eyeglass frames swept up at the corners like wings, the red-faced matron extinguishing her cigarette in a pool of creamy coffee at the bottom of her saucer, these people must not know that I was the child of my parents.

I would pretend to be alone. "But you're too young to drive, how did you get here?" A silent voice posed the logistical problem. "Perhaps I am just a casual acquaintance, a friend, an orphan they brought along for the ride. I will sit with them, but remain silent." An aura of aloofness would disassociate me. I had taken to these inner dialogues, finding conversation with the outside world less reliable. You really laid your life on the line every time you opened your mouth. I kept my own raucous counsel.

As I recall, the crimes for which these three were to be punished by my spiritual abandonment were that they had not dressed for the occasion, that my sister, eight years old, quick-witted and careless, was singing to herself, or ordering a peanut butter sandwich or, upon entering Zip's, had tripped over the untied laces of her red sneakers. It is likely that my parents resembled a Ralph Lauren ad of the eighties, slightly disheveled and sure of themselves. These were easygoing people; I longed for rigid artifice, penciled brows, hair in exotic colors. My father should stay encased in collar and tie at all times. My sister should be staring blankly from a gilt frame at Portraits, Inc. My mother's feet should be bound by high heels, her legs should shine with a second skin of silk and her lower lip should be weighted down into a pout with a heavy layer of Fire and Ice. They should be a 1950s Hollywood family freeze-framed.

I tried to make up for their imperfections, their jokes, their sturdy shoes and oblivious individuality by becoming as fastidious as a grandmother. I had become, in fact, my own grandmother, one more demanding and less forgiving than either of the two that existed in real life. I saw to it that my clothes were perfectly coordinated, I worried over the lack of a scarab bracelet, and hoped, at all times, to create the "right" impression. I watched over my manners as if they comprised my trust fund, my heritage threatened by the callous world at large and by the too-casual family at this table. My tentative hold on a sense of self was threatened by the fact that I was the offspring of imperfect parents, the sibling of a flawed fish from the same gene pool.

Later, as a mother, I was given a few years of grace. Although it would have been fitting had my own early imperiousness been met in kind, I seemed to have been forgiven by the Fates. Maybe I was pretty talented at this mothering business. Maybe I was unique. Maybe kindness and mercy would follow me all the days of my life. Maybe I'd done some good, unremembered but rewarded.

Wrong. At sixteen, my daughter spots my flaws and is as repelled as if I were an ax murderer. My vices: I wear sensible shoes when I should be in stiletto heels, my trousers are baggy where they should be tapered, my ass does not have the resilience of a tennis ball. And, she asks, "Does it bother you that you don't make a contribution?" Contribution. To the world? To the poor and oppressed? To my church? My family? To the Democratic Party? The Parents' Association? I'm scared to ask. Suddenly I don't want to know what she thinks of me. The slight roll of her eyes and the tightening of her lips tell me enough.

This is wartime. Perhaps if one stood behind the aegis of Athena the battle would be endured. Or if one fled on foot a neutral village might offer sanctuary. I know a woman who did just that, the mother of five daughters who walked out the door when her youngest child reached thirteen. She had seen a picture once, in *National Geographic,* of fog rising from a valley in the Blue Ridge Mountains of Virginia. It had stayed in her mind while the babies were growing and as they went off to school one by one and sometimes, even at night, while her husband made love to her, she saw fog and beneath it the deep green of Virginia. "Don't you lay your psychotic problems on me," the sixteen-year-old yelled one day in response to her mother's saying, "I'm sick of cleaning up after you." That seems to have done it. "I need a rest," she told her husband and called the bus station. She asked for information about traveling to Virginia and packed her bag with the ease of one who had practiced this in dreams. A magnifying glass for studying spores, a book into which she would press ferns, a favorite old straw hat with frayed red ribbons that tied beneath the chin, and two pairs of jeans.

They didn't know she wouldn't be back. She may not have known it herself. But there she is and there she plans to stay, in a pre-fab, one-room cabin with a single cot, a Presidential Rocker ordered from L. L. Bean the week she arrived, one coffee mug, plate and bowl bought singly from a local potter, and one fork, spoon and knife. No accommodations for guests and no rebuke.

I am comforted these days by Freud's generous observation that there are two things that it is impossible to do right, govern nations and raise children. It makes it a bit easier to forgive ourselves and our own parents for only doing our best.

It is a cruel blow when children discover that parents, those paradigms of perfection, have warts. Children have to believe in our infallibility because they are at our mercy, their dependence is that of a shipwrecked sailor clinging to a piece of floating mast. What if it were built of unseasoned wood? What if dry rot has set in? What if it breaks in two? For their sanity they must trust that we are seaworthy. We are their real-life movie stars, their heroes until they begin to feel their own strength, until they realize that they are neither shipwrecked nor incapable of swimming to shore. When they need us less, they are free to see us as we are, just as puny human beings like the rest. Until they are certain of their autonomy, that puniness will be feared as a contagion. They must avoid us, literally, as if we had the plague.

I remember that at about the time of the Zip's affair, I told my friend Linda that the people she referred to as Mr.

and Mrs. Lazear were witches who had stolen me from my real parents, who were a king and queen. I guess you know what that made me.

So now my daughter's real mother will put on her sneakers and jeans, not spikes and tapered pedal pushers, and go about her business, occasionally hoping that when the daughter is, oh, let's say twenty for lack of any scientific data, that when she's twenty she'll invite her mother to lunch in some restaurant, not necessarily Zip's Diner, and actually enjoy her company. That she will recant and comment on contributions made is expecting too much. This is, after all, real life. No kings, queens or princesses need apply.

Mothers and Sons

"Mothers raise daughters to be wives,
they raise sons to be sons."
SARAH CRICHTON

You realize, of course, that nothing is going to change until mothers start raising their sons differently. Women can sit on corporate boards, remove cancerous spleens, argue cases before the Supreme Court of the United States, but the heart of man will remain the same. Our presence in the boardroom, operating room, courtroom will be tolerated because failure to do so is considered bad form. But this is a case where form has little to do with substance.

The tolerant law firm will promote women to partnership. The tolerant Port Authority will put Sheila Bloom behind the wheel of a city bus. But this has nothing to do with what the tolerant man is saying of these women when he's having a beer with the guys, and it has nothing to do with how he treats his wife, girl friend, secretary, daughter.

This is the heart of the matter. It is a mother's work to

instill in her sons a respect for and understanding of women. Compared with her, we, the women who come along later in their lives, are limited in how much we can affect men's thinking.

Unfortunately, mothers aren't doing so well. Recently I called on a friend who had to have an abortion, a trauma to heart, soul and body no matter how valid the reason or swift the curette. I arrived with flowers and a bottle of wine, prepared to hold her hand or numb pain with frequently filled glasses. An attractive middle-aged woman opened the door and was introduced as "Phil's mother." It seems that Phil, who was at the office, had asked his mother to accompany his lover to the clinic and to bring her home afterward.

I would wish that that mother had replied, "Look here, Junior, this is a time that you should be standing by." Why did she come running in acquiescence? Because she had too much to lose—her son's gratitude and dependency. Here was a man who thought she was important. She was not about to stand up for what she as a woman knew would be helpful to another woman if she could strengthen the bond between mother and son. Sons are miniature versions of our fathers, the men we first loved and admired. But now there is no mother running interference. Blind love will have its way; over and over again opportunities will present themselves for mothers to teach their sons about women and they will fail to do so.

To us, these objects of a mother's delight are just the men in our lives: the guy who orders two eggs over light, the boss who addresses one as "sweetie," the voice on the other end of the phone saying, "Sell McCrae, buy G.E." Beside these boyfriends, husbands and guys we left behind are mothers whispering in their ears, "I'm always standing by."

Many women seek to have a closeness with their sons that they don't have with their husbands. This is an opportunity to mold an adoring, noncritical fan. I can see the temptation there and I can also see that the waters of "sisterhood" run shallow when the choice is between "sister" and son. These "sisters," other women who will populate our sons' lives in the form of classmates and teachers in the early years, girl friends and colleagues later and then finally lovers and wives, are betrayed by our attitudes.

And it happens in the "best" of homes. In the most liberated of homes. In the best educated of homes. I dined the other night with a friend who is a powerful executive in a major corporation. Her husband is her fan and supporter and her eight-year-old son the apple of her eye. When he appeared to say good night, his mother asked if he had packed for a trip planned for the next morning. "No," was the serious reply. "That's a woman's work." My friend, his mother, laughed.

It's just another example of how we work against ourselves—through communications broad and narrow we do work against ourselves.

Until women truly respect themselves and each other, we will continue to undermine sisterhood through word and example, through the ways we treat our daughters and sons and the way we expect to be treated in return.

Unless daughters are respected, what are sons to think? I know a family that worked hard to win scholarships to private school for their two young boys. They did not feel that the public school was "good enough." Their youngest child, a girl, upon becoming school age was sent to that public school. Not a protest was raised, not a question asked. But what were these parents saying to their boys? That girls are not as important. And this is the lesson with which they will go forth into the world of business, finance, arts, letters and marriage. These are lessons for life.

How odd that at a time when women are demanding more of their husbands, they don't seem to demand more of their sons. What are we turning over to the future generation of wives and lovers and co-workers? Nothing very different from what was turned over to us. Only mothers can change this course of history, can stop its insistent and stubborn repetition. Mothers are the first beloved female in a boy's life. He is like a puppy in his eagerness to please her. He is ready to learn if she will teach kindness, caring and generosity of spirit, if she demands it.

A friend who has five children insists that the three boys partake in all household chores, including the traditional "girls' jobs." She does it, she says, "Because my future daughters-in-law deserve something better." All of our daughters and daughters-in-law deserve something better, but they aren't going to get it until we as mothers start delivering a better and stronger message to our sons. Only then will the species become extinct—that species of head-scratching, muttering men who find it in their best interest to feign ignorance and declare that they just don't know what women want.

Caution! Danger Ahead!

We sit across from each other in the usual coffee shop. The undercooked french fries bear the print of her finger's testing press. With each bite, catchup and pickles ooze out the side of the cheeseburger bun. She licks her fingers, one by one, reassembles and begins again. All so familiar.

How many times have we sat here after school? Five? Twenty? One hundred? How many times have I ordered tea and watched my daughter's adolescent feasting across the table?

But for all the familiarity, today I am a stranger, or she is. It's as if she is on the other end of a rubber band I hold. She stretches it back, back, back, pulling herself out of view and just at the point that I would cringe in anticipation of the imagined snap, she's back again, the elastic slack in my hand.

Not long enough for me to feel that I can reach out and touch her cheek or settle into easy conversation.

It's not the new haircut, although that is, as she says, "more sophisticated," nor is it the surprise of a fully formed body, which like young Tess Durbeyfield's, "made her appear more of a woman than she really was." I don't think my sense of detachment is as much a result of her having "grown up" (whatever that means) as having survived.

Up until this moment I believed that my fears kept her safe, that my tightly woven web of anxiety cradled, secured and bound her. Invisible, invincible threads.

Her gymnastics routines. I could see the disasters. A fall from the high bar, a dismount from the beam miscalculated. A taxi runs a light as she crosses the street. I won't spell it out for you. You're capable of imaginings as gory as mine. Every parent is. And every parent believes that there is magic in the watchful eye. As long as it sees it saves.

What is overwhelming about the birth of a child is not the miracle of conception, gestation and delivery. That course has been charted for all to see. Public television will take you from Petrie dish to the first pop of an emerging head. No. The real mystery, the real source of awe is that the universe changes the moment we look into those new eyes. The world becomes a frightening place. There is danger out there, making a determined, unswerving path in our direction.

Reason begins to slip away. Every reported disaster becomes our own imagined possibility. There was a week once in the park when the nannies disappeared and were replaced by nervous mothers. It seems that the previous weekend a neighborhood infant had been drowned by his deranged sitter. A house burns in Newark and we check three times to make sure the stove burners are off before we retire for the night. A sniper strikes in Nashville and we would fashion bulletproof vests in children's sizes. Statistics of adolescent victims of auto accidents become film strips that run through our brains. Only in these the victim is ours, the blood spilled is familiar.

Anything can happen, and does. Today the New York *Times* reported that two Columbia College students picked up a carpet on the street and got quite a surprise. You can imagine the scene: a perfectly good carpet there with the garbage, they hoist it to their shoulders and stage a march triumphant back to their room. Police Lieutenant James McKenna told the reporter, "They thought they were going to decorate their little dorm room, then they unrolled it and found a body."

And just like that the horrors roll on. For instance, in this year alone: A urologist allowed his fourteen-year-old child to assist in an operation. Some fifty-year-old woman is walking around with a fourteen-year-old's handiwork in her bladder. A man married his mother after her fourth divorce. He says he didn't know who she was. She knew who he was, all right. Little children at Public School 203 were watching a Laurel and Hardy movie when a few feet of pornographic film flashed on the screen. A chicken was arrested in Maine, and zoologists shipped a pregnant baboon off to impregnate another baboon. And I should be sanguine as I send my daughter into the world? I should keep my head when all about me are losing theirs?

Ah, but the cautionary tale will keep her safe. Words of warning, like the watchful eye, will keep such things at bay. "Look both ways before crossing." (This to a sixteen-year-old.) "Don't drink from public water fountains." "If you eat a hamburger cooked over oleander twigs, you will die." It's hard to cover all the eventualities. With the birth of a child we realize the true extent of our helplessness. It hardly seems fair that no sooner do we fall in love with this new creature than we have to hand it over to the vagaries of fate.

I wonder what my own mother was thinking as I, a six-year-old, walked out the door and headed for the school bus, separated from her gaze by trees, a hill and whatever imagined catastrophe. Did she wonder, "Will I ever see her again?" Did she believe that it was an invisible amulet fashioned from her worries that brought me safely home each night? Lunch box in hand, I was free of fear. It was high adventure out there in those woods.

Of course there is no proof that worries, the watchful

eye, the cautionary tale don't work. You know the joke about
the lady who explains to her psychiatrist that she tears up bits
of paper to keep tigers off the New York City streets. "Well,
it works," she tells him. You can't argue with that.

But you can argue that imagined woe has never kept
anyone safe. My daughter sits here licking catchup from her
fingers as though nothing has happened. And that's the point.
Nothing has.

There comes a time when we are no longer the guard-
ians of our children's safety. One day we think we are still
carrying them and then we realize they have disembarked.
It's a bit like feeling pain in a phantom limb.

At some point they begin to operate under the same
principles as the rest of us. They do look both ways before
crossing. They do drink from public fountains but they don't
lick them.

We become dispensable. Not in the ways of slick new
razors or hospital thermometers or plastic straws. We have
left more of an impression and we would be missed. But the
job was done before we knew it.

The cheeseburger is finished. Red-stained napkins are
heaped on the plate. My daughter leans back. "So then we
went out to dinner and to a disco." At once I begin to envis-
age the dangers that lurk in that particular neighborhood.
But my voice is stilled. She has, after all, lived to tell the tale.

On the Road
with the College Applicant

My sixteen-year-old daughter slumped against the doorway of the college admissions office. "It happened," she groaned. "I had a stress interview."

She exhaled as though she'd been holding her breath for the previous forty-five minutes, and sank to the ground, risking grass stains on the carefully selected, conservative interview skirt that must appear the next day on the next campus. "The minute I walked into his office," she explained, "he demanded, 'So! What can you do for this college?' " The tone she captured sounded like that of a police interrogator— "Were-you-or-were-you-not-at-the-scene-of-the-crime-the-night-of-the crime?"—a tone that tempts one to admit guilt in order to be free of the questioning. "Then it turned into a game show. If I responded the way he wanted me to, he'd say, 'Good answer! Good answer!' " She looked at me with astonishment, "And *then* he said, 'There's an invisible box on my desk with things in it that describe you. What's in the box?' "

"What did you say? What did you do?" I asked anxiously, the beats of my heart quickly catching up to the race of her own. Did she black out? Did she excuse herself and go to the bathroom? Was the course of her future determined by five minutes of silence?

"I went on automatic pilot," my daughter responded, adding, "In a stress interview, you separate your mouth from your brain and hope it works."

Later the adults in her life become witty, bright and piercingly intelligent over the food and wine of a family dinner. With a safe distance between ourselves and the Ivy League interrogation chamber, with a safe distance between ourselves and our own tremulous youth, we sound like Bartlett's Familiar Quotations. We are not struggling to describe ourselves with objects that could fit inside an invisible box. There are no cold sweats, stutters, blushes or stammers here.

Her grandfather says, "When he asked what she could do for the college, she should have said, 'What can your college do for me?'" Another diner suggests, "She should have looked him in the eye and said, 'If the point of an interview is to become acquainted with the applicant, why are you determined to make me ill at ease?'" A wise guy notes, "When he asked what was in the box, she should have said, 'Your head!' and walked out."

Easy for us to say. Smug as we are with degrees under our belts. She, on the other hand, can't afford the luxury of brashness nor the time to change the system. Chances are she'll even apply to and pray for acceptance at the source of the stress interview. It's a seller's market. College-bound high school seniors can rattle off admissions statistics the way they once might have memorized batting averages. Numbers culled from college catalogues march through their brains: "In 1984 approximately 12,636 applications were reviewed for 1,360 places in the freshman class." SAT scores, CEEB scores, AP scores and grade point averages join the parade. It keeps them up nights.

Lack of sleep and fear of rejection take their toll. My daughter has become crazed. Every high school senior I know has become crazed. One of them told me that she thought it was a trick question when her interviewer asked her one balmy August morning, "It's such a lovely day, would you like to meet outside?" Another became so nervous that he lost all sense of spatial relations, and after pulling up a chair across from the interviewer's desk, he promptly sat on the floor. When it was time to leave, he walked into the closet rather than out the door. My daughter tells me that she is certain, "When the interviewer asks you where you want to sit, your choice MEANS something." Even successful interviews are belittled in the general mood of overwhelming pessimism that the students adopt, in part to protect themselves from what they perceive as inevitable disappointment.

There's perversion at work here. Applicants begin to assume that the harder it is to get into a college, the better that college. And they, who happen to be at the age of least self-confidence, feel they couldn't possibly be "good" enough to be acceptable. Admissions committees aggravate this sense of insecurity by flaunting the number of applications they receive, statistics of which they are justly proud— statistics that reduce sixteen- and seventeen-year-olds to a sense of barely tolerable inadequacy.

I watched an applicant walk onto the campus of one of the "hardest to get into" universities, look around at what appeared to me to be no more than the normal sampling of collegiate scruffiness, and remark fearfully, "Look at all those geniuses!"

"It's hard not to feel victimized," my daughter tells me. "Even when it's not a stress interview, these are strangers probing into your life, and you didn't invite them there." Some interviewers are sensitive to the intrusive nature of their jobs and the vulnerability of their "victims." At one of the most competitive colleges an admissions officer, upon shaking my daughter's hand and finding it cold said, "Let me make some coffee to warm you up." If an applicant is in a position to decide, decisions have been based on less than that.

They're also based on the personality of the tour guide and some sort of Rorschach reaction to the appearance of students and campus. While admissions officers are seated in the position of power, they are not alone in the seat of judgment. Applicants come equipped with the ruthlessly critical eye of adolescence. I have heard hundreds of years of academic glory dismissed in a sentence:

College A "is full of preps."

College B "is like Coca-Cola, they spend more money on their image than the product."

At College C, "The students are refugees from Westchester going native in L. L. Bean boots."

College D "has gone commercial with the quota system. They make certain to show you a specific number of jocks, brains, wimps and weirdos."

College E "was great! The guy who interviewed me was a Mets fan."

Chance encounters also make an impression. My daughter and I were having a pre-interview lunch in College F's cafeteria when a student walked in with a Steiff bunny rabbit puppet on her hand. She spoke exclusively through the rabbit. When another student asked, "How are you?" the bunny's head bobbed up and down to the lilt of a Walt Disney cartoon voice, "Just fine, thank you." I promptly addressed the tuna fish sandwich at hand, but caught a glimpse of my companion rolling her eyes.

It doesn't look good for College F.

However, in spite of the stress, the defenses, the critical eye, there are moments of love at first sight. Such events are unpredictable except that they hardly ever happen on rainy days and rarely on Saturdays when one senses the interviewer's annoyance at having to work weekends. For my own daughter, these moments occurred when an interviewer lost track of time and talked with her for two hours, when she met with a Classics professor who had the tenderness and wisdom of Catullus behind his eyes, and when she dined with a professor who shared her passion for Shelley and Keats.

And that is supposed to be the point of all this—passion. The goal of higher education is to seduce students into a love of learning, to nurture and encourage a lifelong love affair. The root of the word "education," comes from the Latin *educo*—to bring out or lead forth. It seems that both applicants and admissions personnel lose sight of this in a system that has become rife with stress, statistics, slick catalogues and superficial encounters, that has created a kind of painful endurance test for parents and children. I wonder if colleges are even aware that admissions procedures have placed intimidation and interviewers' invisible boxes before their gates? And that many will stumble there, many who should be brought in, in order to be "brought out."

Babies' Asses

My husband and I have been thinking a lot about babies lately. The hot, moist smell of babies fresh from naps. The clasp of searching fingers encircling one's own. Giggles rising up from protruding bellies where kisses land. Last night I dreamed of firm baby ass in my right hand as my left patted its way to a burp. My husband murmurs into the steam of his breakfast coffee, "Maybe we should adopt an orphan."

It's springtime and I'm nostalgic for the equipment of the young; tricycles, plastic motorcycles with their sirens removed, marbles, jacks and strap-on roller skates. I miss the creature who once practiced with all of these for hours until she got feet and wheels to work together and felt the euphoric forward surge of movement. Man was driven to discover the wheel in order to experience just such joy.

"I'm so sad to think that it's coming to an end," says he, and I am surprised for a moment to realize that this is not a mother's private domain, this mourning the loss of infancy, childhood, the dependencies and intimacies of our last child whose desk is now piled with college catalogues, whose hours are spent on the phone, calling out. Conversations with the outside more often than around our dining table. "Hello, out there." Preparing the way for the time, little more than a year from now, when for her, "out there" will become "here." The places she and I call home will eventually be different, as they must be. And I dream of babies' asses.

If anyone had ever told me in my pre-motherhood years that one falls in love with one's children, I would not have understood. Would not have understood that they meant in love, something different from loving. I probably would have imagined that that sort of thing happened in Rome where I remembered children and parents in streetside cafés, strolling hand in hand through the piazzas after dinner. If an infant cried, it was swooped out of distress onto a sleek Valentino silk shoulder. Parents shared looks of adoration over the tops of their children's heads, looks that could have been lifted right out of the paintings in the Vatican collection, looks that said, "This is our treasure." In Rome, I would have believed it happened. But here, on these cold puritanical shores? Here in my own home?

Nothing could have prepared me for the first instincts on wet contact to smell, lick and touch the newborn. No one could have described and made sense to me that in later months, when infant and mother would be separated by job or nightfall and different rooms, that it would feel as though a limb were missing. And certainly I would have turned away discreetly if they had spoken of the later years, of "favorite songs" and places that would become "our" favorites.

I began to get wind of it in her seventh year when my child left to vacation with my mother in the seaside summer home of my own youth. I had taken a break from the work that kept me city-bound and away from fogs and salt airs, and had wandered into "our favorite coffee shop." Something was wrong. The coffee lay in sullen bitterness beneath an iridescent slick, the guys behind the counter smoked while they fried eggs, squinting against the fumes wafting up from the corners of their mouths. Their fingernails were dirty.

Had there been some mistake? Was I in the wrong place? And if not, what had been our mistake in considering this place a prize? It was clear, of course, that it was "favorite" because we had made it our own through shared observation and conversation, had made up lives for those we watched walk by outside on Madison Avenue or those sharing tables whose routine badinage would be embellished by our own. Without her, the place was a dump.

Like being in love with a lover, being in love with a child colors things. You aren't to be trusted. Everything is a bit more than it seems. Everything seems a bit more than it is. If you are fool enough to speak of it and another is polite enough to listen, he will smile and change the subject. It's like telling your dreams—not polite conversation. The listener wonders if you know how much you've revealed. Did you mean to lift the hem of your soul and have him peek beneath?

But unlike being in love with a lover, you know from the start that this love object is a fledgling, here to learn how to leave. From the first rush of infatuation, the movement is away. What is left when the movement is completed? A somber plain of bad restaurants and sentimental songs? I can only imagine it now standing as I do on this side of experience, imagining empty space full of sayings that don't get said, hours when there should be a presence and there is none. Will I envision that presence as I did my dog's after he died? I would trip over open air where once he had lain dreaming of whatever it is that makes dogs twitch and whimper in sleep. Several times I entered that vacated space catching my steps in order to avoid the fall over fur and bone, the fall over a phantom. My stomach would lurch up as it does when you step down expecting one more stair than exists at the end of a staircase. You've touched bottom and don't know it.

We're thinking about babies, my husband and I, and I'm watching mothers with grown children. I want to know, what brings them home? Whose children enjoy the company of parents? It seems that many offspring return on unacceptable terms. There are the seductive parents who make life with them so enticing, so sympatico that their children are unable or unwilling to strike out on their own, to become adult, to create their own happy marriages and families. They are kept in a state of perpetual dependence, the parents' one way of ensuring that they'll stick around; tar babies of sorts. A friend of mine who was building a summer home said, "We're going to put a wing on for the children, to try to seduce them into coming to spend time with us." Would they have been doing these "children," in their twenties and thirties, a favor if they had given them L. L. Bean sleeping bags and suggested they take up backpacking instead?

There are the polite families. There were never fights over dinner. When adolescence arrived, none of the raw and hurtful acting out of that period took place under the family roof. None of the necessary "I hate yous" were aired, followed by a morning wash of, yes, but I also love you. When they might have learned about each other, parents and children were keeping hostilities at bay. Years later they retain a polite distance, reaching out occasionally as one does in the hope of being known and loved, reaching out in spite of the fact that the scenario is familiar, that there will be disappointment followed by a retreat into superficial interaction, a simulacrum of sympathy.

And then there are the children who keep coming around to finish unfinished business. Who, at twenty-six, forty-six, fifty years of age are still trying to reroute themselves to avoid the pitfalls. Their reunions begin with eager faces and end in tears. There are follow-up phone calls and letters. Family patterns are as fixed as mazes in old English gardens. You'd have to dig up a lot of boxwood before you could change it. Tradition, habit and the way things take root will keep it in place.

The child of the needy parent returns out of a sense of guilt and duty as if paying his tithes for the right to work a separate plot of land, for autonomy. He comes calling and thinks of other things, focusing his eyes on the parent's, hoping that the glaze over his own will hide the absence of solicitude.

I think those who return unencumbered, of their own free will, are those whose parents didn't collapse in the wake of departure. Their marriages weren't held together "for the children," and their lives are full in spite of the fact that one of its most fulfilling phases has ended. Children probably return home for the same reason that any of us visits anyone. We prefer the place where we will be comfortable and at ease, have a good laugh and receive solid advice. Lucky parents. Lucky child, when it works.

To be able to create such an atmosphere is a gift. Is there anything more important we can guarantee our hostages to fortune as they graduate and move on? I can hear them now, "Yeah, you could give me a BMW. A summer in Europe would be better. A string of pearls . . ." Something to be wrapped and shared with a friend. Something to show for it.

Did I do it right? As I think of babies I ask that bombshell of a question. Were we honest parents? Did we hang in there? In the passion of our loving did we lay the cool, matter-of-fact foundation of trust? If we started again, easing the pain of leave-taking with the prospect of new arrival, would we love better? Does anyone ever learn to love better? It would probably be the same. I'd fall in love, the time would fly, and before I knew it, I'd be thinking that this was some sort of a trick, some sort of bad joke. I'd smooth our days with affection, fill the air with kisses and compliments and in the tradition of the best of lovers, make the loved one feel so confident that she would know she could survive without me. She would return the favor by doing just that. And once again, I would spend my nights floating through dreams of babies' asses.

Boys and Girls
at Play

No Girls Allowed
(and This Means You!)

"Girls won't do!" the *maître d'hôtel* stammered. "Won't do what?" my friend the tax lawyer asked. "I think he means you can't eat here," her client, a man, translated, and led her from the grill room of a Wall Street eating club.

Another lawyer tells of her most recent luncheon meeting at a men-only club. "I was overcome by an irresistible urge—no, more like a calling—to run around the dining room licking all the silverware. She surmised that it would have to be thrown out after it had been contaminated by a "girl."

She's wrong. Those kitchens come equipped with two machines. The blue one for boys is a standard commercial dishwasher. The pink one is an autoclave.

Women make men very nervous.

Perhaps you've noticed the bad case of nerves recently suffered by members of the Century Club, a men's club in Manhattan, when it was suggested that sisters join the brotherhood. If you have been mystified by the response, it is only because you perceive Centurians as the grown-ups their titles imply. This is where you have gone astray. Do not see them as partners in law firms, writers who win literary awards, critics who determine how we are to read poetry and prose. See them as eight-year-olds guarding their tree house.

Surely we can remember wanting to be members of those childhood clubs—offering to pay double the penny dues, to steal cookies from our mothers' kitchens, to tell dirty jokes—anything that would persuade boys to lower the ladder for us to ascend to that mysterious male haven between the leaves of trees, held up by branches and the fear of girls.

We were told that we could not join because girls:

1. Can't throw a ball.
2. Giggle.
3. Are stupid, and anyway,
4. Wouldn't understand.

I always wondered "understand what?" and assumed that it had something to do with reproduction or baseball cards. I'm not convinced that it doesn't.

What is that "pleasant, if not always cosmic, communion," of which George W. Ball speaks? Whatever it is, there are many gentlemen who state that admitting women "would drastically change the nature" of this communion and "break down the effortless, unconstrained companionship which over the years has characterized the Century." Baseball cards.

Perhaps you fell for the disguises—the watch fobs, pinstripes, wingtips and occasional boutonniere. I'm sorry to have to inform you that those came from the grown-up costume trunk at Central Casting. You thought they were real. "A club like the Century should surely be unaffected by fashionable whims—such as those directed toward eliminating all the delightful differences of the sexes," a minister told us. You thought you should be charmed because he termed the differences "delightful." You stopped to wonder if desire for acceptance was a "fashionable whim." After all, a real grown-up was telling you so.

Keep your eye on the ball. Remember the eight-year-old. Remember the tree house. I tell you, there is no difference. Do not be thrown off by the fact that these are people of learned counsel, who number among their membership famous civil liberties lawyers who have fought for the equality of the outcasts of this earth.

Consider an alumni dinner that my husband attended many years ago at a prestigious medical center. None of the women graduates were present. When he inquired as to their absence he was informed: "We don't invite the women. If they were here we couldn't tell dirty jokes."

Keep your eye on the ball. Don't focus on the fact that these are the men who remove cancerous organs and gangrenous limbs, who replace arthritic hips with Teflon and breast tissue with silicone. Remember the eight-year-old.

More often than not the disguise will carry the day. But men still fear that we'll see them as they feel they are. This is understandable. After all, they've been given important work to do: save souls and after-tax dollars, send troops to El Salvador and nuclear satellites into space, run major corporations and money-lending institutions; write best sellers and monographs on the workings of the mind. They must keep out the spies, women who will see through the pipe smoke and gray beards and will hear the whispers stretching forth from wing-backed leather chair to wing-backed leather chair:

"Do you have a Dave Winfield?"

"Yes. Do you want a Reggie Jackson?"

"Good! Let's trade."

Of course, the other reason that they would exclude us is that they need a break. Relating to women wears them down. We try these finely tuned minds, and men don't care to be befuddled. Consider Henry James's nineteenth-century club man Colonel Assingham, who regularly retreated from the complications of marriage to the undemanding simplicity of his club. "This was the way he dealt with his wife, a large proportion of whose meanings he knew he could neglect.

The thing in the world that was least of a mystery to him was his Club."

It puts a strain on them that we insist that our meanings are not to be neglected. They retaliate. If they are forced to comprehend the incomprehensible workings of our minds then, they insist, we must accept and understand the obscure peregrinations of theirs: that women should not join the Club because "it never occurred to the founders that women might become members." It also never occurred to the king's tailor as he stitched the required buttons to the coat sleeves of the royal guard (to discourage them from wiping their noses thereon) that with the advent of Kleenex men would still demand those buttons.

Since women are in the business of understanding, we oblige—to a point. We understand but do not accept. In fact, we understand more than they would like. We understand that this is the playground. No more. No less. This is recess time when boys were liberated from overheated classrooms they were forced to share with girls, and from the humiliation they were forced to share with each other, that girls were better at reading and handwriting, manners and cleanliness. What a relief to throw oneself into fresh air and packs of exclusivity, to run faster and throw farther than any girl. They could exercise their male instinct and neglect those confining qualities of grace insisted upon by the females in their lives.

Within the Club's walls the male ego can be stretched without snapping. But once women join their ranks, the men know that the "spirit of brotherhood which has prevailed and should prevail in our lovely institution" will be threatened by members vying for women's attentions. Remember how boys would beat up other boys on the playground if some pretty girl were there to impress?

As we return to the playground, to the tree house, to the eight-year-old to understand this current skirmish, we can also return to the nineteenth-century mind. Substitute the words "membership in men's clubs" for "literature" in the following letter from a Mr. Southey to Charlotte Brontë upon receiving her poems: "Literature cannot be the business of a woman's life, and it ought not to be. The more one is engaged in her proper duties, the less leisure will she have for it, even as an accomplishment and a recreation." There are certainly nineteenth-century echoes in the voices of protesting Centurians.

My fourteen-year-old daughter says of Mr. Southey, "Obviously he was threatened." Obviously.

Sorority Rush at Ole Miss

There's no white trash here. No hillbilly, red-neck or peckerwood daughters. No hicks, grits, haints (from "haunt," a girl described by boys up North as a "dog" is a "haint" down South), and certainly not a Snopes in sight. If one slipped into Ole Miss, you can be sure she wouldn't be rushed by Chi Omega or Delta Delta Delta, home of the well-born and the blond. Polishers of the jewels of Southern womanhood.

An "active," as distinct from an "alum" or "rushee," has the freshly scrubbed, squeaky-clean prettiness featured in fifties movie magazines. The wholesome, small-town gal who had been "discovered" and was to become a star; who came from a nice family, wanted a husband and children—for whom she would give up her career, of course; a churchgoer and the fierce guardian of her own virginity. She's here today at the University of Mississippi in Oxford.

The Chi O's and the Tri Delts have spent their summer preparing for seven days in August when they will compete for more of the same. They will rush those entering freshmen who have won the most beauty contests, good citizenship awards, highest grades, and praise from sorority alums in their towns.

What those alums see and say matters. "Mississippi isn't a state, it's a club," says one of its citizens. "It's amazing what people know about each other." A girl had better watch her step if she, as the heroine in F. Scott Fitzgerald's "Bernice Bobs Her Hair," longs "to join the starry heaven of popular girls."

And a starry heaven it must appear. Chi O is first in academic achievement and claims as alums Miss Americas Mary Anne Mobley and Linda Lee Mead. The rush chairman (no chairperson here, please) is the most visible member and an advertisement for what you can become if you become Chi O. She's beautiful, sweet, sincere and plans to go to law school. She is also Pi Kappa Alpha's 1984 National Dream Girl. There's a tiara and an engraved silver tray to prove it.

Entering the Tri Delt house is like entering a cage of canaries. They're so blond, so soft, so bouncy and high-voiced. Good will abounds.

But don't think they're dumb. Don't for a minute think that. One of their professors notes, "They're not going to rattle off Emerson's Divinity School address even though they know it. That's not charm."

Charm is everywhere. So is hair. It dips, it swirls, it cascades. It's a Walt Disney cartoon. You remember Snow White's and Cinderella's hair. It defied gravity. It floated like meringue above their heads. The only difference here is that BMW's and red MG convertibles rather than golden coaches and white steeds set these damsel's tresses flying on night air.

Who knows where they buy their clothes? One suspects an underground couturier who only services the upper middle class Mississippi maiden. Demure sundresses reveal a trace of ladylike breast. Floral patterns in fuschia, magnolia, pale pastels. Each complements the other. Each looks just right in the lavender light of August, against antebellum brick, beneath the heavy green of cedar. Their toes end in rose petals; the nails, painted a pale pink, peek from delicate sandals.

If a blemish ever had the audacity to appear on this creamy skin, it would be removed from view by a steady, well-trained hand. "Puttin' on makeup is just somethin' we learn to do. We all watched our mothers sittin' at their dressin' tables."

There's a Walt Disney lilt to the voice. If an "active" burst into the song "Someday My Prince Will Come," no one would bat an eye. Chances are a tear would be shed. After all, that's the business they're in for the next seven days. All the sororities will stretch out tentacles of tender manipulation and envelop the nubile maidens arriving from the Delta, the coast, the piny woods.

From Yazoo, Calhoun, Greenville, Tupelo, Indianola, Laurel, Natchez and Jackson come these Lauries and Lories, Missies and Cissies, Pebbles and Pipers, Winters and Teras to put their lives on the line. They know that the sorority they join will determine their futures, their social standing and the man they will marry. They know that "desirable" fraternities, those whose members are "intelligent, good-looking and ambitious" don't go courting Zetas. They are ripe for what's to follow.

Open House or Ice Water Parties on Saturday. Three days of Coke Parties followed by Skit and Pref Parties, each more exclusive than the one before. Freshman dorms are rife with rumor. "I've heard if you're handed a Coke and you don't ask for a straw, you won't get invited back." "My cousin spilled lemonade on her dress and was cut from the Skit Party."

The rushee's fear is matched by the active's sincerity. She is sincere through eleven Open Houses, nine Coke Parties and seven Skit Parties, all leading up to the biggest show of sincerity, the Pref Party. Her smile does not fade. Her dimple only deepens.

Each party begins with the hot, perfumed flesh of actives

pouring forth from the sorority house to envelop the trembling limbs of the assigned rushees. Once inside they engage in high-pitched sounds in accordance with the pamphlet *Conversation with Rushees*. One sorority suggests the following: "DO look for common characteristics—or for opposite ones. (Example: 'Your hair has so much body! Mine's so hard to fool with in this weather . . .')" . . . "DON'T ask the Rushee if her watch is really a Rolex."

Whatever it is they are saying, some are saying it on their knees. They look deep into the eyes of the rushee sitting above them and implore and beseech with a combination of courtliness and calculated passion befitting a nineteenth-century suitor.

Meanwhile the knife of judgment is sharpened for the plunge. Each night's voting determines which girls are "in" and which are to be cut.

At Tri Delt the rushee's fate depends on whether the "Poop Groups" find that she possesses "creativity, good looks, intelligence, popularity, loyalty, friendship, thoughtfulness, honesty, leadership, individuality, athletic ability, high ideals, scholarship, compassion."

Over on Rebel Drive the Chi O's consult the poster they've placed on the wall to remind themselves of "Good Adjectives" and "Other Adjectives." Those who fit the "good" category will be invited back. That is, if they are "amusing, appreciative, captivating, clever, dainty, dazzling, congenial, refreshing, zestful, talkative." It's curtains for the girl who is "icy, glacial, vain, smug, pretentious, insensitive, immature, fidgety, aloof, boastful, babbling, gushy, sharp, shallow."

Two who have survived and will be invited to the Chi O Skit Party were high school student council members and class officers, cheerleaders and "class favorites." They were both listed in *Who's Who in American High Schools*. One was "Most Beautiful" as well as being a "Lions Club Sweetheart" and "Future Farmers of America Local and District Sweet-

heart." The other was a DAR Good Citizen and had straight
A's. Both daddies were in business. (Daddies who once
would have been planters are now car dealers.) Their mamas
were Tri Delt and Chi O. One had three Tri Delt cousins, 2
Phi Mu cousins, a Phi Mu aunt and a Phi Delt uncle, not to
mention a Delta Psi dad.

Skit and Pref will put the survivors through their emotional paces. Do they cry because they are moved or because
they are away from home for the first time? They are quick to
assure you, "These are happy tears." One rushee notes,
"They seem to put the girls they like best in the front row so
they can make them cry."

"We NEVER try to make them cry," protests a Tri Delt
officer. "I know that at some sororities they say, 'Make them
cry! Make them cry!' But we never do that. We cry because
we're so moved." They are moved each time they perform
the seven skits. Few can finish the Delta Love Song, "This
special feeling can be yours. Believe in it, the flame is lit, By
Tri Delta love, with Tri Delta love, In Tri Delta love."

Chi O saves the Big Cry for last, for Pref night when
they've narrowed the field to those rushees they really want
and might lose to Tri Delt. They send them away sobbing.
They themselves occasionally wipe a perfectly dry eye. But
what they can't wring out in emotion, they deliver in effect.
The Chi O girl is a beautiful, well-oiled machine. She could
be in the Museum of Modern Art's design collection.

She serves up a sexless sexuality. Although she's all
bump and grind and black net stockings during skits, her
smile reminds you, "This is an act, this is what I can do if
called upon." This is when she shows her legs, her looks, her
cool wit. It is Pref night when she reveals her "true self," her
humanity, a certain softness of heart and gift for sentiment.

As evening falls, the Chi O's, in matching white formal
gowns, assemble to welcome the tremulous rushees. On the
patio, punch, tea sandwiches and guile are served with crystal, sterling and antique lace. The mood grows somber, the

light fades, the mellifluous voices sing and wobbling white high heels ascend the staircase. Here, in the parlor in the midst of flowers and candles strategically placed by local alums who've worked all day creating the atmosphere, sad songs and heartfelt speeches are sent floating out to a cacophony of sniffles.

A song of Chi O friendship is sung to the tune of "Bridge over Troubled Waters." "Where Is Love?" is asked to the melody from *Oliver.* The answer is that it's here in Chi O. "It's nice to know there are sisters . . . when there's no getting over that rainbow." A memorial of sorts to Karen Carpenter, who sang the original version and only had a brother; a reminder that although the flesh is weak and the spirit falters, a sister is always a sister.

Then a voice that had belted out Broadway tunes the previous night comes in on a whisper and a prayer. "Each of you is so special and you mean so much to us. I hope you know. We have such a wonderful sisterhood here. Tonight each of you must make a decision that will affect your life greatly. Search your heart. Your heart will know. Tonight you'll find a home. A place for you. Tonight." When there's no getting over that rainbow, a pregnant pause helps.

Here comes *West Side Story.* "There's a place for you . . . hold my hand and we're halfway there, hold my hand and we'll take you there . . ." That does the trick. By the time they leave to go to two other parties, the rushees are falling into the arms of those who in the late hours of this night will decide their fate.

One suspects that the tear and hug factor has something to do with who will get bids. As the Chi O actives line up outside in the darkness to bid them farewell, some rushees get hugs from ten, some from twenty and some only from the home-town girl or cousin who sponsored them. It doesn't look good for the girl in the sequined shoes.

As I depart with the rushees, two alums swoop down upon me like the buzzards one sees in Mississippi skies.

"Were you interviewing those rushees?" Cherries in the Snow lips stretch over tightly clenched teeth. "The girls are very concerned that you might break the spell they've worked so hard to create." Not a chance.

The Tri Delts are sexier than the Chi O's. Look at Pepper. Look at Jordan. Their skin has a golden gleam achieved by "layin' out on the roof." Jordan's blond hair, as soft and yellow as an Easter chick's, and her small gently curved body are used as exclamation points in her conversation. A toss of the head, a slight bend of the knee, a giggle.

Pepper's pose consists of one hand on a hip, one at the back of the head and an outward thrust of healthy buttock. She fastens on you with sleepy brown eyes and you begin to wonder, is it true what they say?

If you buy the sincere report of all actives and rushees, then you have to believe that the sorority system at Ole Miss has the largest concentration of maidenheads ever assembled in one place. I'm not sure how such things are measured (how many hymens can dance on the head of a pin?), but some sort of record is being set here. "It's very important to the Southern man that his bride be a virgin," they tell me at Chi O.

"Right," confirms a visiting alumnus, a member of Sigma Chi fraternity. "That's why at thirty-eight I'm still a bachelor." It's breakfast at Smitty's. When you're a grown-up and have business on the Square in Oxford, this is where you gather before opening shop. A natural progression from the frat house. It's convivial, and by 7 A.M. the air is as thick with talk and laughter as the molasses poured over hot biscuits.

"Now, you see," adds his fraternity brother, "it's more like a case of regenerating virginity. If you're in love and do it, you're still a virgin. 'You're trash, you sleep with your boyfriend.' 'No I'm not, I'm in love.' If you do it in the woods you're still a virgin. And if you get pregnant you're still a virgin because it obviously wasn't premeditated."

Another good ole boy joins the table, drawn by the delight exuded by Southern men when they're making fun of the womenfolk, those creatures who have somehow gotten the upper hand throughout their history together. "Do you know the one about the Confederate monument on campus?" he asks. "The soldier tips his hat at every passing virgin."

Who knows? Who cares? But if she's caught, "She'd have to turn in her badge. Anyway, a Chi O girl wouldn't do that," asserts one of their members. Neither would a Tri Delt. "We don't have that kind of problem because we get a quality girl." And that quality girl had better come to them whole, chaste and pure.

If she doesn't, there's hell to pay in the bid sessions. There will be somber murmurs, "Questionable rep," "Happier elsewhere," and the girl is cut. Not for her the sweet success of membership and elitism. The information comes either from a home-town girl or an alum. Among other things, a questionable rep results from "dating a boy six years older" as well as having "gone too far." "The poor girl from Oxford," moans one rushee. "If there's a skeleton in her closet, there's bound to be someone to drag it out."

But if she's lucky, on Sunday night when the rushee joins her colleagues at Fulton Chapel to receive her bid, she learns that she is to be inducted into this society of vestal virgins who guard the flame of Southern ladyhood. She runs down the hill of Sorority Row or Rebel Drive into the waiting arms of her sisters-to-be. If she has gotten a bid from one of the less desirable houses, she walks slowly. If her bid is from the sorority the guys call "the haint house," she may just stay fixed in place and do what she's done all week. Cry. No one will suspect because all along she's been saying, "These are happy tears."

Some Thoughts on Growing Up

Middle Age:
Becoming the Person
You Always Were

I wish I could remember who said that in middle age we become the person we always were. I think it might be so. In fact I feel it happening. Bits and pieces of self, discarded in adolescent frenzy or early adult preoccupation, seem to be floating downstream and fetching up on my shore. I imagine that when I reach middle age I will be a rock covered with moss borne by spores on the wind and lichen brought by who knows what. At any rate, it will all be familiar. We'll all nod to each other—the rock, the moss, the lichen, the visiting toad and the perching dove and say, "Nice to see you again." And then we'll settle in to stay.

I've heard others comment on these rumblings, these soft shifts in the soul's crust. Such a stir occurred yesterday before I even knew it. That's how it happens, before you even know it; the way you feel a mild tremor only after the fault has parted and meshed together again.

It was a gloomy, damp day. Out of nowhere, or so it seemed, came the idea that I must head directly to the Metropolitan Museum of Art, cross the hall, ascend the staircase, go straight to the Monets, stand and stare. It seems that I thought if I stood long enough, the apple blossoms, gardens, lavender poplars and azure skies would float out of their frames and into me, like ice surrendering to water. Perhaps all that Monet fecundity would crowd out February weariness. Well, of course. Why else do people visit museums?

I had avoided them for years, following a girls'-school education that had featured art appreciation—not to be confused with art history—as an intricate step toward becoming a lady. You can't carry your pedigree around with you, our trainers reasoned, but you can acquire certain graces and knowledge that will let the world know. If I remember correctly, these included, in addition to appreciating art, holding a teacup properly and never eating on the street. Somewhere along the line they merged and became confused with the general discomfort of wearing stockings. I rebelled.

The fracas of the adolescent heart also dispensed with organized religion. As soon as it was no longer a daily requirement, I refused to go to church. I closed out all memory of comfort or peace found there, the fun of singing hymns louder and higher than the next guy, the soothing familiarity of the *Book of Common Prayer.*

Lately I find myself in church and am surprised each time —not knowing why I came, or quite how I got there, but feeling familiar and singing my head off.

It's very odd to have parts of the self rubbing up against one like a cat.

In her essay "Aces and Eights," Annie Dillard writes, "I am 35; my tolerance for poignancy has diminished to the vanishing point." I would like to ask her, "So how is it at thirty-seven?" If it's not too late, I'd better warn her. I'll tap out the code on a tree trunk or put a note in a bottle and toss it into the East River. In either case the secret will be carried from Manhattan to Tinker Creek. "Pardon the intrusion, Miss Dillard, but I thought you ought to know that in middle age the heart becomes a goldfish."

If you have ever had the misfortune of holding a gold-

fish in your hand, you will know what I mean. There is a wet
and desperate thrashing. Unprotected for contact with anything as firm as knuckle and callous, its vulnerability beats
against the inside of your fist. You know that your thumb
would leave the imprint of its press. If you squeeze too hard
the fish will bend and die. If you hold too lightly it will fly
away, remembering in midflight that it is wingless. Life! Life!
is the code its tail beats out against your hand. Holding it
makes you squeamish, letting go is no choice.

It's not like catching crickets or flies or lightning bugs.
They will protest because, like the rest of us, they don't
choose to be contained. But their angry stampings are not the
same as a squirm for dear life.

If you held a stethoscope to the closed fist grasping the
fish, I imagine you would hear a sound similar to a fetal
heartbeat. A wet message from another world.

It seems that as we become the person we always were,
our hearts return to what they once were. Squirming, wet
and wingless, sending the message through the wall: Life!
Life!

I don't think we knew the "person we always were"
when we were being it. It's like negative space. When you
look at a David Smith sculpture, you don't know which ex-
cites you more—where the steel is or where it is not. We
don't experience the negative space until time and age have
thrown up enough of a structure to give it something to
scratch its back against. "Oh, here I am," we say as the familiar floats by and decides to stay.

For some, becoming this person is no more, or just as,
complicated as becoming one's own mother. I had the fortu-
nate or unfortunate occasion to witness this when I returned
for my prep-school reunion. Here is Sarah, who once upon a
time had distanced herself from the image of her mother by
strict dieting, increasing the space between them by decreas-
ing her own. Now, eighteen years later, she stands beside

me, large and bluff, putting the same strong arm around me that had once made her cringe.

And here is Louise with the thin-lipped reserve that had elicited the comment sixteen years ago: "My mother is an iceberg." Now I feel as awkward as Louise herself once felt before this slick of perfection, this perfectly formed icicle.

But as I was saying, I had felt the urge to go to the Metropolitan Museum and had raced up the stairs to get to the top before closing time. I would like to tell you, Annie Dillard, that there was a "poignant" moment, a reunion of sorts between the *Path in the Ille St.-Martin* and me. But in fact, the guard at the door said, "We're closed, miss."

Perhaps the race rather than the getting there was the most important part of this story anyway.

So, when it comes, I imagine that middle age will find me as a craggy rock, rough-edged toward the sky and smooth where my base touches water, where rivulets warm in the sun and tadpoles sleep until the next rush of water brought by rain or winds; a sometimes-churchgoing radical who doesn't eat on the street and is mad for Monet.

Naming Things

Each Sunday I read "Sky Watch" in the second section of the New York *Times.* K. L. Franklin, astronomer emeritus of the Hayden Planetarium, instructs readers to hold his star map vertically. The outer circle represents the horizon and the center of the map the zenith. Then you look up. Then you lose your way.

On the chart, stars are flat black circles attached by lines to form constellations. There's Boötes, Draco, Lepus and Eridanus, easy to behold within the confines of newsprint and my room. But outside, in the expanse of night, stars refuse to lay flat against the sky. They glitter, they tease. Other stars intrude into my appointed constellations, rogue stars unaccounted for by Dr. Franklin. Uninvited dazzlers flicker like bedizened young girls stealing the show from the guest of honor. Constellations rarely appear as they are described. The sky is an ink blot. Make of it what you will.

Manhattan is not the place for stargazing. Lights and pollution dim the view and caution prevents staring upward too long lest you, with chin pointed toward heaven, be caught off guard by wanderers of the night out for things earthly rather than celestial.

The truth is, I don't do it much. We're at dinner during prime time, or I lack the patience for peering. I know this each week as I clip Astronomer Franklin's map, even as I read the humor and poetry in his words, "Now that the moon is no longer in our way . . ." learn his amazing facts, "The Big Dipper is not a constellation but an asterism, the technical term for figures that have an identity of their own but are part of a larger constellation." Just like the rest of us. Sometimes he sounds like a man in love, like a sixteenth-century poet in love, "This week even the bright full moon cannot hide the mystery of Sirius . . ."

The mystery of Sirius, the mystery of nodding trillium, the mystery of chuck-will's-widow, they're all the same. They comprise my protean perimeters. If you check the weather page of the daily *Times,* you can find out when Jupiter, Mars and Saturn are rising, not because you plan to be there, but because it is, as they say, what's happening.

Next week, in the Great Smokies, the National Parks Department is conducting a "wildflower pilgrimage." I like the department's choice of words and dream of joining the quest, of clearing calendar and conscience long enough to spend three days kneeling for a closer look at green shooting forth through the dark and forgiving soil of Tennessee.

My sister, who knows her trees, who can identify birch, willow, oak and maple by bark, limb, trunk and leaf, wants to teach this to children. Her plan: to point to one child and ask another, "How do you know that this is John?" The child, if all goes according to plan, will respond, "Because he has blond hair and blue eyes." My sister, the gratified teacher, will then move from eyes to branches, from hair to foliage. I love the idea and I'm afraid it won't work. Children, those supreme narcissists, are interested in children, because that's what they are. They are not interested in trees except to the extent that plant life interferes with the normal course of childish things-tangles a kite string, stands in the path of a careering tricycle or drops a baby bird, dead and featherless, its open beak emitting ants rather than song. Then they take note, not of the tree but of its crimes.

First, second and third grade nature walks. Wet feet, cold, boring. "All we do," my friend Linda reported home, "is step in cow plops." We did not join our teachers' enthusiasm for identification. Jacks-in-the-pulpit and lady's-slippers were the only names that stayed in our minds because their blooms were so blatantly sexual. Clearing grasses away for a better springtime view of snowdrops, bluets and violets was not something I did then. It's something I do now.

I've joined that group of grown-ups who stop their cars to stare up when a hawk is spotted overhead. We know all the while that identification is impossible from this distance, but we feel compelled to bear witness. I have become a caresser of trees. It's okay, most people can't tell, it's not so unusual to allow one's hand to rest casually on a trunk. But my hand is neither casual nor resting, it's trying to learn the sense of trees. This will come in handy if I am ever blinded. And in the meantime it's a way of becoming acquainted, or raising a hand in a sign of peace. This isn't kids' stuff.

When I was eighteen I knew a woman who dashed from her house whenever she imagined the call of a yellow-crowned night heron. Pulled forth by an obsession to sight the creator of that cry, she would haul her oversized body across rocks and sand to the shore. She read nature books while she ate, leaning forward over the table, one hand holding her chin, the other guiding tuna salad from plate to mouth, sometimes continuing the motion even after the food was finished. We called her "The Bird Lady" and dismissed her as a bit dotty.

Another bird lady of my earlier childhood was elderly and fed chickadees from her lips. She would secure a sunflower seed between the puckered pink slices of flesh and raise the hull heavenward. Dark brown seed, pale rigid lips, white hair framing it all. Silence. And then the sound of wings. A few passes and a chickadee would make contact, plucking the seed from her face as if she were the flower itself, top heavy and mute with seeds. I never trusted her after that.

My own daughter has her apprehensions. She asks my mother if a growing interest in birds signals the onset of menopause. Her facetiousness is not beyond reason. The most passionate gardeners, bird watchers and stargazers I know are men and those women who are unable or have ceased to conceive. Their focus extends beyond the immediate domestic to vast natural perimeters, as if in celebration of a boundless fertility unaffected by menarche's clock or a partner's whim. In celebrating, they sing the names of things.

A christening of sorts. "And what will you name this child?" the minister asks. With the utterance of that name, the infant is promised the protection of a greater being and the possibility of life everlasting. His world begins to close around him and hold him up. By naming him we have said, we take you seriously. It is a mark of our appreciation and seriousness of purpose. It bespeaks our good intentions.

The summer brings wildflower bearers, triumphant with their colorful catch captured and held in jelly jars. The needle-breadth stems of white snakeroot, yellow adder's-tongue, tall hairy agrimony, horned bladderwort and hairy skullcap collapse, unaccustomed as they are to stares through glass. I often wonder, would they have been spared if their villainous sobriquets had been known? Probably, partly out of distaste and partly because naming things is a form of possession. "Hmm, a broad-lipped twayblade," we murmur and move on. *Nos morituri salutamus.*

I suspect that in the end, a sense of mortality leads us to name things. We want to know where we have been and with what we have shared the sojourn. We want to connect with star lives measured in millions, with pearly everlasting pushing its way through soil each spring whether or not we are there to see. We are reassured by continuity, by the osprey, identical to its parents and the parents before that, heeding its timeless lessons in survival, building nests in dead trees and fishing summer lakes. These are the things that festoon our way, our going out and our coming in. We might as well shake hands and get on with it.

Hello, Out There

The Dirt Eaters

"Southern Practice of Eating Dirt Shows Signs of Waning"
(New York *Times,* Monday, 2/13/84)

Who knows what the dirt eater knows? According to *Times* reporter William Schmidt, slave owners muzzled them. Not uncommon in the face of the primitive or the truth. But who is to say theirs is not a sense of place?

Babies know. Surely you've seen them crawling beneath your glance, pink mouths pursed and pressed against a veil of mud. It's how they get to know a place, begin to feel at home. We have a harder time feeling at home. Rambling wanderers, foundation pourers, skyscraper builders going higher and higher to put down roots.

Fannie Glass is quoted as saying that she misses it most after a rain, "When the earth smells so rich and damp and flavorful." Arthur Miller once described that scent, "earth as air." That sweet raw smell of early spring.

A sense of place. Ask the most regional of writers about it and they become vague. "Well," they try to explain, "you know everyone and they know you." Sometimes there are no words—just a taste in the mouth.

Philip Johnson speaks of the spirituality of place. There is no proof that he means its buildings, although that is his business. As he aged, film director Luis Buñuel bid adieu to the places he loved, places where he had lived and worked and to which he knew he would never return, he said "goodbye to everything—to the mountains, the streams, the trees, even the frogs." And W. H. Hudson in his autobiography, *Far Away and Long Ago,* wrote about the "head of an ancient and distinguished family," the owner of one of England's famed country houses, whose "greatest pleasure was to sit out of doors of an evening in sight of the grand old trees in his park, and before going in he would walk round to visit them, one by one, and resting his hand on the bark he would whisper a goodnight."

Johnson, Hudson, Buñuel have known what the dirt eater knows, that this is more than architecture and plantings, this sense of place. They have known that when the land is moist and fresh it puts a hold on you. Grabs you by the gut, by the palate, some would say by the heart, and won't let go.

Fannie Glass's husband doesn't understand. "It makes your mouth taste like mud," is all he'll say. "I wish I had some dirt right now," is her response.

So do I, and I know just where I'd go. Not to make a feast of it, but to make it mine in ways acceptable to those who trained me—with dollars and cents, liens and easements, and covenants running with the land.

The dirt eater knows you can carry a place with you. William Schmidt reports that Dr. Sidney A. Johnson, a rural physician in Goodman, Mississippi, "noted that fine clays have a tendency to adhere to the lining of the intestines." What Dr. Johnson does not note is that it also has a tendency to adhere to that silky smooth lining of the mind that determines passions of the heart.

Passion is what it is. The dirt eater knows this although

he may not tell you or Dr. Johnson. Passion—not a matter of diet, minerals, trace metals, nutrients. "Researchers say those who eat dirt do not do so to satisfy hunger or to meet a biochemical urge . . ." Researchers are stumped.

They have found, and don't know what to make of the fact, that shoe boxes full of the stuff are sent up north to relatives who "crave the flavor of dirt dug from clay hills back home." When I was in boarding school, my mother used to send me shoe boxes of bread, fresh baked and packed with cheese. She didn't know it was dirt I craved, that the smell of the land and its soft touch beneath my back had made its claim. That I had felt the slow shifts of grass giving way to soil giving way to China or whatever lies beyond roots and worms and moving moss.

Perhaps if I had carried it away in the lining of my intestines, perhaps then I could have staved off the yearning. Perhaps if I had developed a taste for the land in the fashion of Fannie Glass, perhaps then I could eat from a jar that held my favorite piece of the old sod. Earth as air. Stomach as heart.

Dr. Dennis Frate, a medical anthropologist from the University of Mississippi says, "As the influence of television and the media has drawn these isolated communities closer to the mainstream of American society, dirt eating has increasingly become a social taboo." Media, slave owners, Levittowns, K-Marts would make a sense of place a social taboo.

But the dirt eater hears that muffled call of the land. The dirt eater knows that beneath parking lots and shopping malls, concrete, glass, asphalt and cinderblock the land awaits the moist and gentle touch of tongues.

If a Bomb Is Dropped on Pomfret, Your Desks Will Save You

Once a week a distant wail floated down the halls of Pomfret Community School and we were instructed, "Boys and girls, climb under your desks. Put your hands on your heads. If a bomb is dropped on Pomfret, your desks will save you."

Other than some doubt that hands the size and weight of tuberous begonias could save our eight-year-old heads from the crush of a bomb, thought and conversation gave way to stupor during those routine air-raid drills of the 1950s. Unlike fire drills, which shot us forth into fresh air and instant mania, the air-raid routine set us in stillness. Strange silence fell over third-graders otherwise compelled to fill space with stink bombs, water bombs, cootie catchers, peashooters and any dirty joke about reproduction.

As we went forth into the sixties with passion and words as weapons against napalm, pollution, body counts, the ABM and the DMZ, few of us remembered that silent denial of terror or the vulnerability of small bones bent beneath desks.

We became "adult" in the seventies without connecting our frantic need to be all things in one lifetime to an awareness that the lifetime could be very short. We would insist

that each hour be lived as fully as a day, each month as a year.
We would be accomplished poets as well as physicians, mothers as well as lawyers, master carpenters as well as computer
analysts. We would feel rootless and fail to see that our roots
grew from a deeply buried, insidious awareness of the bomb;
that bomb of our childhood.

It becomes clearer as one air-raid-drill generation begets
another. My young daughter and her friends recently returned, rosy-cheeked and distressed, from a carol sing at a
neighborhood nursing home.

"I hope we aren't like that when we're old."
"We won't be. We will keep each other company."
"We probably won't be old."
"Right. We'll probably be killed in a nuclear war."

Tonight that same daughter asks, do we know that there
is a fallout shelter in her school? It has been there since she
began kindergarten eight years ago, but today she noticed.
"Do you think that there will be a nuclear war?" Her question pleads for a lie for an answer. I oblige. But later, at
bedtime as blankets tug her to safety, she adds, "I'm scared."
I want to respond, "Me too." Our children's fear is as conta-
gious as a yawn.

Suddenly I imagine my tall husband, my daughter and
myself in that third grade posture, crouching to save our
lives. This time, however, my hands shelter the heads of
these people that I love, and this time I know that hands
before a bomb are like butterflies before a gale.

On television our children saw Reagan flying home from
Texas on the airplane that will soar him above nuclear disaster. They heard him speak of the possibility of "limited" nuclear warfare, and saw disbelief strike their parents' faces like
a slap. They have begun to harbor their own versions of our
third grade horror fantasies.

Cynicism, manic denial and barely contained violence

will be theirs as it was ours. The "sixties generation" and the children of the eighties share a common disaster . . . coming of age in a world that constantly reminds them of the possibility that they might not come of age; a world in which the possibility of annihilation hovers as calmly and insistently as a black cloud bearing a squall across the bay.

Unborn Baby Roe and the Born-Again Right-to-Lifer

You may have seen the photograph outside Grand Central Station or inside airport lobbies. If it caught the corner of your eye, chances are you thought it was Vermont in the fall, so rich the reds and golds. On closer inspection ribs emerged. Butterfly antennae netted midflight and pinned with a drop of raspberry jam. The posture, curved in the momentary shape of a beckoning finger, and the eye, larger than the ear beside it, finally form a whole and an identity. An aborted fetus in 8″ × 10″ Kodacolor for the world to see.

When they aren't bombing clinics, pro-lifers assault the senses. "It was a boy, you know." The woman's voice, fearful for its anonymity and the hour, announces a fact she could not know. What she does know is that the person answering her 2 A.M. phone call had an abortion the previous afternoon and will be distressed by these words from the avenging angel of the unborn, this pro-life spy, a nurse planted in the abortion clinic.

Dr. Bernard Nathanson, a renegade abortionist, lauds *The Silent Scream,* a documentary film of a fetus being aborted, as an opportunity "to see abortion from the victim's vantage point." As if "victim" were singular and easy to know.

I came of age before *Roe* v. *Wade,* the Supreme Court's 1973 decision, made it possible for a woman, within specific guidelines, to procure an abortion for her own rather than the state's reasons. In those pre-Roe days it was not difficult to identify the victim.

Teenage girls would disappear from the small rural community where I was raised. "Gone to live with an aunt." They would return several months later, listless and changed. There was a scent of shame about them from which we recoiled. We understood nothing, but as children, we had an unerring ability to sniff out dishonor.

There was no reinstating them into our lives. No intervening years or subsequent legitimate children, no amount of churchgoing or Christmas caroling would make them one of us. They might as well have been the defiled Tess returning to Marlott a century earlier.

Later, in college, rumor and paranoia were rampant. Over dinner, forks would stop, suspended before gaping mouths, as news came of a classmate missing since a scheduled weekend rendezvous with an abortionist. Of course, there was the alternative. We all seemed to know at least one eighteen-year-old who had left Shakespeare, Blake, Marx and Freud behind on her desk in order to set up house, await a baby and divorce. The survival rate was not high for these marriages begun in surprise, based on alarm and invaded almost instantaneously by a stranger not chosen.

Information was communicated in whispers while eyes darted about for possible eavesdroppers. There was a purported physician in Pennsylvania whose own daughter had died during an illegal abortion. As a result, the story went, he had given up legitimate practice to tend to others' daughters. I never knew whether this man existed, bearing his curette like a cross.

The rich girls went to Puerto Rico and those without money or connections went into lonely labor in dorm rooms. No one ever asked what became of the infants. This was wartime except that the blood was shed ingloriously.

We learned very early that society considered us dispensable. That there was a cruel, collective conscience exacting punishment for a woman's sexuality. Of course our classes taught us that there was nothing new in that. We had read of Calypso abandoned on her love-tossed bed, releasing the virile Odysseus to his virtuous Penelope; of unchaste Tess spurned by a husband who loved his ideals more than his bride; of the flower-bedecked Ophelia and Jean Rhys's Mrs. Rochester swallowed by madness. What was left for Tolstoy but to silence Anna's libido with the wheels of an oncoming train?

Nor was there anything new in others laying claim to a woman's body. From Hellenic times when women became chattel, to Hollywood in the fifties, to Brooke Shields's mom. We assumed that someone somewhere had a superior right to ourselves.

This is the world to which clinic bombers and 2 A.M. phone callers would relegate us. This is the world advocated by those who recently marched on the Supreme Court to mark the twelfth anniversary and protest the imagined ignominy of *Roe* v. *Wade.* Neither rage nor reason are gender specific. The marchers were male and female and it was men who sat on the bench in 1973 to give something of women back to women.

Laws do not change people. They merely determine the extent of their suffering. In the years following *Roe,* we did not witness a rush of profligate womanhood, nor, if the decision is overturned, will we usher in an era of celibacy. Men and women will continue to fall in love. Caution will be struck mute by loudmouthed Passion and the woman will half-expect to be punished for it. That is her legacy.

And her fact, if she becomes pregnant. I know of no

woman who comes to abortion without ambivalence or who fails to experience mourning in the aftermath. She does not need the pro-lifer to raise her consciousness. Hers is not a decision made in a moment of caprice. A woman finding herself pregnant does not simultaneously experience a metamorphosis into Lady Macbeth. Although the pro-lifer would have it so, she does not approach the clinic with cunning and a cold eye on murder. "Murder" is his term used to envision and cast the woman as villain rather than victim. An ancient ruse.

And a clear transference. His bombings tell more than he would like; that he is pro-violence, pro-punishment, pro-death. His ideals more precious than life. He would bomb mothers to save fetuses. Which is not to say that he is not well-meaning. Just as Angel Clare was well-meaning when his adherence to principle led to the execution of his tainted Tess.

The real "danger" he guards against is a woman's self-determination, the possibility that she might be less passive before cruel fates and few alternatives. The "enemy" he would destroy is a woman's sexuality, despised since Helen and accepted only if harnessed by a husband and kept from view. In the fetus the pro-lifer has found a "victim" worthy of his vengeance. Like a "good" war or a public hanging, it legitimizes the killing instinct.

If the law is changed as a result of his hysteria, women without "connections" will simply go back to coat hangers, poisons and unlicensed physicians. What the pro-lifer will get for his efforts is two corpses instead of one.

Of course, in the best of all possible worlds, women would become pregnant with just the number of babies they could care for. Babies would be swaddled in cotton and bedded down in bassinets rather than bagged in polyurethane and dropped in dumpsters. They would be pushed to the park in perambulators, not found floating downstream, bruised and lifeless.

But in the world as it is, women will continue to seek abortions and there is no guarantee that they will abort for the "right" reasons, just as there is no guarantee that they will marry, take lovers or have babies for the "right" reasons. But these are matters for heart and conscience, not state and vigilante.

If *Roe* v. *Wade* is to be overturned, we will hand our daughters the society inherited from our mothers and grandmothers. One that teaches them, as we were taught, not to take themselves seriously since they are not, after all, the final arbiters of their existence. They will learn, as we did, that in the most intimate relationship with themselves, they will be without choice or that given illegal choice, they are dispensable.

The Box Man

The Box Man was at it again. It was his lucky night.

The first stroke of good fortune occurred as darkness fell and the night watchman at 220 East Forty-fifth Street neglected to close the door as he slipped out for a cup of coffee. I saw them before the Box Man did. Just inside the entrance, cardboard cartons, clean and with their top flaps intact. With the silent fervor of a mute at a horse race, I willed him toward them.

It was slow going. His collar was pulled so high that he appeared headless as he shuffled across the street like a man who must feel Earth with his toes to know that he walks there.

Standing unselfconsciously in the white glare of an overhead light, he began to sort through the boxes, picking them up, one by one, inspecting tops, insides, flaps. Three were tossed aside. They looked perfectly good to me, but then, who knows what the Box Man knows? When he found the one that suited his purpose, he dragged it up the block and dropped it in a doorway.

Then, as if dogged by luck, he set out again and discovered, behind the sign at the parking garage, a plastic Dell-wood box, strong and clean, once used to deliver milk. Back in the doorway the grand design was revealed as he pushed the Dellwood box against the door and set its cardboard cousin two feet in front—the usual distance between coffee table and couch. Six full shopping bags were distributed evenly on either side.

He eased himself with slow care onto the stronger box, reached into one of the bags, pulled out a *Daily News* and snapped it open against his cardboard table. All done with the ease of IRT Express passengers whose white-tipped, fair-haired fingers reach into attaché cases as if radar-directed to the *Wall Street Journal.* They know how to fold it. They know how to stare at the print, not at the girl who stares at them.

That's just what the Box Man did, except that he touched his tongue to his fingers before turning each page, something grandmothers do.

One could live like this. Gathering boxes to organize a life. Wandering through the night collecting comforts to fill a doorway.

When I was a child, my favorite book was *The Boxcar Children.* If I remember correctly, the young protagonists were orphaned, and rather than live with cruel relatives, they ran away to the woods to live life on their own terms. An abandoned boxcar was turned into a home, a bubbling brook became an icebox. Wild berries provided abundant desserts and days were spent in the happy, adultless pursuit of joy. The children never worried where the next meal would come from or what February's chill might bring. They had unquestioning faith that berries would ripen and streams run cold and clear. And unlike Thoreau, whose deliberate living was self-conscious and purposeful, theirs had the ease of children at play.

Even now, when life seems complicated and reason slips, I long to live like a Boxcar Child, to have enough open space and freedom of movement to arrange my surroundings according to what I find. To turn streams into iceboxes. To be ingenious with simple things. To let the imagination hold sway.

Who is to say that the Box Man does not feel as Thoreau did in his doorway, not ". . . crowded or confined in the least," with "pasture enough for . . . imagination." Who is to say that his dawns don't bring back heroic ages? That he doesn't imagine a goddess trailing her garments across his blistered legs?

His is a life of the mind, such as it is, and voices only he can hear. Although it would appear to be a life of misery, judging from the bandages and chill of night, it is of his choosing. He will ignore you if you offer an alternative. Last winter, Mayor Koch tried, coaxing him with promises and the persuasive tones reserved for rabid dogs. The Box Man backed away, keeping a car and paranoia between them.

He is not to be confused with the lonely ones. You'll find them everywhere. The lady who comes into our local coffee shop each evening at five-thirty, orders a bowl of soup and extra Saltines. She drags it out as long as possible, breaking the crackers into smaller and smaller pieces, first in halves and then halves of halves and so on until the last pieces burst into salty splinters and fall from dry fingers onto the soup's shimmering surface. By 6 P.M., it's all over. What will she do with the rest of the night?

You can tell by the vacancy of expression that no memories linger there. She does not wear a gold charm bracelet with silhouettes of boys and girls bearing grandchildren's birthdates and a chip of the appropriate birthstone. When she opens her black purse to pay, there is only a crumbled Kleenex and a wallet inside, no photographs spill onto her lap. Her children, if there are any, live far away and prefer not to visit. If she worked as a secretary for forty years in a downtown office, she was given a retirement party, a cake, a reproduction of an antique perfume atomizer and sent on her way. Old colleagues—those who traded knitting patterns and brownie recipes over the water cooler, who discussed the weather, health and office scandal while applying lipstick and blush before the ladies' room mirror—they are lost to time and the new young employees who take their places in the typing pool.

Each year she gets a Christmas card from her ex-boss. The envelope is canceled in the office mailroom and addressed by memory typewriter. Within is a family in black and white against a wooded Connecticut landscape. The boss, his wife, who wears her hair in a gray page boy, the three blond daughters, two with tall husbands and an occasional additional grandchild. All assembled before a worn stone wall.

Does she watch game shows? Talk to a parakeet, feed him cuttlebone and call him Pete? When she rides the buses on her Senior Citizen pass, does she go anywhere or wait for something to happen? Does she have a niece like the one in Cynthia Ozick's story "Rosa," who sends enough money to keep her aunt at a distance?

There's a lady across the way whose lights and television stay on all night. A crystal chandelier in the dining room and matching Chinese lamps on Regency end tables in the living room. She has six cats, some Siamese, others Angora and Abyssinian. She pets them and waters her plethora of plants —African violets, a ficus tree, a palm and geraniums in season. Not necessarily a lonely life except that 3 A.M. lights and television seem to proclaim it so.

The Box Man welcomes the night, opens to it like a lover. He moves in darkness and prefers it that way. He's not waiting for the phone to ring or an engraved invitation to arrive in the mail. Not for him a P.O. number. Not for him the overcrowded jollity of office parties, the hot anticipation of a singles' bar. Not even for him a holiday handout. People have tried and he shuffled away.

The Box Man knows that loneliness chosen loses it sting and claims no victims. He declares what we all know in the secret passages of our own nights, that although we long for perfect harmony, communion and blending with another soul, that this is a solo voyage.

The first half of our lives is spent stubbornly denying it. As children we acquire language to make ourselves understood and soon learn from the blank stares in response to our babblings that even these, our saviors, our parents, are strangers. In adolescence when we replay earlier dramas with peers in the place of parents, we begin the quest for the best friend, that person who will receive all thoughts as if they were her own. Later we assert that true love will find the way. True love finds many ways, but no escape from exile. The shores are littered with us, Annas and Ophelias, Emmas and Juliets, all outcasts from the dream of perfect understanding. We might as well draw the night around us and find solace there and a friend in our own voice.

One could do worse than be a collector of boxes.

The Voyage Out

Playing After Dark

I have just read about a cruise of the ancient maritime silk route. The ship, with a heavy, heady ballast of anthropologists, ornithologists and art historians will hoist anchor in Singapore on April 6, 1986, and spend a month sailing to Athens via Bombay, Burma, Madras, Sri Lanka, Yemen, Luxor, Jordan and Cairo. At some point, whether while passengers are aboard or on land beholding ruins left behind by the greed of antiquity no different from our own, Halley's Comet will pass overhead.

I want to be there and have been unable to think of anything else. Like Hamlet, I am beset by logistical and emotional quandries and pulled toward madness, feigned or otherwise, by passion and obsession.

A month at sea when my daughter, a high school senior, will be hearing from colleges? She will need a mother to join in her happy celebration or to incense her with assurances that these things always turn out for the best. Decisions for her future will have to be made. And I at sea? I swept up by the heavy perfumes and sweaty masses of a Persian market? I feverish and tossing with "turista" while decisions are to be made?

It would be unkind. And yet, I begin to remember my own April when choices were made. Receiving the news in a boarding school mailroom far from my mother. I have no memory of sharing my decision or the admissions committees'. It was the beginning of my own life. But is a mother who hungers for a sight of Halley's Comet on its return voyage from the sun the same as a mother who has set distance between herself and her child for purposes of that child's better education? I think not. At least in the latter case, abandonment could be justified on both sides.

And yet, I am certain that to turn one's back on life or to squint at its brilliance rather than facing it with eyes held open is ungracious. Like a child who opens a birthday gift and barely glances at it before reaching to unwrap the next. Someone's feelings might get hurt.

But I also know that of all things, we vouchsafe to keep our children from harm. Will my daughter feel betrayed? Will she, who must stay behind to attend school, think, "If she really loved me, she would not leave me at a time like this." That charge, that one does not love sufficiently, can never be disproved. It is a standard that exists only to serve the purpose of suffering.

There is, on the other hand, no question in my mind as to what my husband's response would be should I head off to follow ancient routes and stars. How odd that it is easier to predict adults' emotional reverberations. After all, we were children once. But the cloak of amnesia that smothers all memory of pain in childbirth falls over that child after birth so that as adults, it separates us from memory of childhood suffering, muffles the cries and makes empathy more difficult. We might risk breaking our own hearts otherwise. But my husband's reaction I can anticipate. He, whose job, unlike my own, does not allow him to disappear into adventure and time, will be sad. He will miss me. He will, at times, be angry and wonder whether, upon my return, he will be able to forgive my month-long abandonment. He will be noble and wish me godspeed. I will worry that he will ease loneliness in the arms of another. I will not worry that love will cease. I am most concerned that in my own rush toward the light, I might make his life grimmer.

I am becoming a stranger wandering in the midst of these intimates of mine. I move among them muttering silently like a zealous convert. Singapore-Bombay-Athens, Singapore-Bombay-Athens takes up the beat of a Gregorian chant or nursery rhyme, repeating itself, taking on a life of its own and determining the tempo of my steps. These people with whom I share three meals a day, an occasional bottle of wine and caresses so familiar that without them we feel shipwrecked, these cherished ones have no idea that as I go through the motions of domesticity, my mind is that of a convict mapping the underground route from cell to open air beyond the gates. I will dig my way out with a spoon cached at lunch. I will move the earth by spoonfuls and by night. I will grovel among earthworms and roots, returning to march in the yard and work in the shops by day. A model prisoner. A model prisoner standing on a foot of soil under which is open space.

These, my dearest friends, do not know that as I plant the garden, plan dinner parties, forget to call the painter, remember to take the clothes to the cleaners and the dog to the vet, that while I am asking the butcher for chicken breasts, skinned, boned, split and pounded flat, that I am dreaming of Halley's Comet. Is this how Anna felt when Vronsky first touched her passions? Will my husband feel like Karenin even though my leave-taking is temporary and not for another? Whatever. My mind is that of one engaged in an illicit affair, anticipating the hot joy of encounter while tucking in the ironed cotton sheets of the marital bed.

And yet, how do I convince myself that I am neither convict nor adultress? How do I learn that eagerness for experience is not the same as "getting away with" something? That it's not blasphemy to cry out, as the protagonist in Mark

Strand's short story of the same title, "More Life!" My yearnings are not the roots of heinous crime. Before I can keep those I love from feeling feloniously assaulted, I must convince myself that I am not a felon.

When I was a child, one of my favorite games was "Mother, May I?" "Mother," chosen from among us, would face a line of fellow eight-year-olds standing twelve feet away and call out, "Samantha, you may take one giant step" (or baby step). If Samantha forgot to ask, "Mother, may I?" she forfeited her forward progress and returned from whence she came. The goal was to be the first to reach the place where "Mother" stood. You would be surprised how many of us forgot to ask permission. We resisted, even then.

Of course, the grandest triumph of all, the one anticipated with shaking hearts and the nervous smiles of frightened children, was to sneak forward unnoticed and without consent; to take baby steps so small or giant steps so swift that they eluded detection. It was the suspense and the desire to practice our ability to move ahead through prowess rather than permission that made us gather players at every recess, on Saturday mornings, after school and best of all, after dark. Playing after dark made our movements easier to conceal. "Mother's" sense of what was and what appeared to be became fuzzy at dusk. Tree shadows blended with those of our own limbs and the primitive fear of night heightened the thrill of subterfuge.

Those frightened to risk the surreptitious step, who dared move forward only by permission, usually came in last. Those who perfected the smoothness of masked movement, who stretched their toes forward to gain an inch, who tried to ignore the butterflies in their stomachs, imagined with each step that "Mother" shouted, "Gotcha!"

Thirty years later I still anticipate that cry.

It's possible that we're as eager to be the monarchs as the subjects of permission. I remember now that the prize for the child who came in first was to be the next "Mother." How many prisoners dream of becoming wardens? How many sinners cops? How many tortured students teachers? Identification with the aggressor gives life an order of sorts. Back then, in our game, it kept things under control. It helped keep down potential insurgents. It discouraged those who might have determined that the real adventure was to break out of the game, to wander off and play alone after dark.

Halley's Comet will be seen only by those who play after dark.

The Journey as
Solitude

I have a friend, happily married, who says that she can't imagine leaving her husband for another man. What she can imagine is leaving him for solitude. It's harder to win than a lover, but it may better nourish the soul.

If my friend left, her husband might find it hard to believe that it was a quest for solitude rather than sexual adventure that called her away. Jason, who believed that Medea's grief would be cured by lovemaking, was not the last of his kind. It is not unusual for men to view sex as a palliative and its absence as the explanation for unrest. The derision of other men is imagined. "If he were giving her good sex, she would stay put." What they fail to understand is that sex, "good" or otherwise, is like salt on a bird's tail. Contrary to primitive belief, it does not ground one. Touch does not tame the urge to soar.

It is understandable that these sons of Jason would find it difficult to comprehend that daughters of Medea, so different from themselves, are capable of cravings for silence as ferocious as their own for sex. If a woman had the choice of a

week without solitude or a week without lusty encounter,
chances are she would elect the latter. Given the choice.

There is a tree in our park favored by birds, a mysterious
choice without leaves or berries in these early days of March;
yet every evening at five-thirty, it sways with the ruckus of
sparrows and finches. If you sneak up on them they don't fly
away, but fall into a silence so thick, you imagine their
breathing. This tree reminds me of a woman's life.

We welcome the hubbub and resonance of other lives,
unfold our limbs to support and hold them. The air around us
fills with chattering distraction. We encourage intimacies,
bask in companionship, tales, details, news. We were the first
to tell our children stories and then listen when they returned
the favor. We taught them the pleasure of repartee and
charmed them with our company. They were trained to seek
us out, to gather round our tables, settle into our laps. We are
flattered by the attentions of men, by the aging Sartre's report to Simone de Beauvoir that he could only talk to a man
for a short period and then didn't care for a repeat perfor-
mance; ah, but to talk with women, that was a different matter. There's a lot to be said for being needed. Being the
caretaker of others' souls gives one a sense of purpose and
worth. A tree is less a tree in the absence of birds.

And yet, as the business of others' lives gathers round,
settles into our branches and begins to hum, we long, at
times, for silence, not as the absence of din—something to be
acknowledged and contended with like the breathing presence of birds—but for the absence of the singers themselves.
We long to be separated by a sea or plains, mountains or
river, to put the distance of the road between ourselves and
those whose melodies we can't resist, whose choruses we
join, drowning out ourselves in the uproar.

It is a need to find and sing our own song, to stretch our
limbs and shake them in a dance so wild that nothing can
roost there, that stirs the yearnings for solitary voyage. To see
ourselves against the backdrop of antiquity, reflected in for-

eign ponds and rivulets undisturbed by those whose movements ripple the water and refract our images in familiar streams. It is to discover that we are capable of solitary joy and having experienced it, know that we have touched the core of self.

The branches of the tree in my park are gnarled and bent to the earth. Ice storms or the weight of birds? The bodies of old women, when seated, curve into the shape of a lap; sinew, bone and tendon molded and informed by the lives they've held.

The other day I saw a photograph of Mauritanian nomads standing on the Road of Hope. Tall and straight as though stretched between sky and desert, they stood within loose-fitting gowns ingeniously designed for ease of movement, for travel. The hot and blustery wind lifted the fabric and sent it billowing toward the horizon. I imagined and envied their lives, imagined worldly possessions packed up and moved on without a moment's hesitation. No checking the social calendar, no canceling orthodontist appointments, no considering whose feelings might be hurt that one had pulled up stakes rather than showing up. I imagined warm winds rushing up legs, past naked buttocks, chest and neck to send out a garment like a banner.

The nomads reminded me of a mother swan I saw one August day on an island pond. She floated before her tiny troop of cygnets, fluffed her feathers, folded her wings to form a spinnaker, and held herself passive before the wind, submitting to its design and fetching up on the opposite shore. One by one her disciples did likewise. A game for a summer day. A lesson in how to move on.

It's good to know how to move on, to gather silence about one like a summer breeze, to spread the wings and embark on the solitary journey, submitting to its ways with the grace of the swan, the ease of the Mauritanian nomad.

The Journey and Childhood

Few traveled from the intimate rural community in which I grew. My friends' parents were farmers whose paths were set by the animals they kept. Out to the pasture, into the barn, dinner at five o'clock in dark kitchens smelling of woodsmoke, barnyard and rare roast beef. Those silent beings about the table were faceless to me in the way that a child is aware of the possible threat or comfort of adults, but not the adult self.

However, there is one face that emerges from memory, the face of a man I will call Mr. Pierson the Adventurer. "He works for the state," his daughter had told us. The state. That impressed. It had a ring of authority to it, like monarchy and kingdom, something bigger than we could see with eyes, something more exotic than the ordinary things we knew in daily life. Mr. Pierson plowed the roads.

No child went to bed on a snowy night without thinking of him out there, surrounded by darkness and gathering snow. It was the loneliness and unpredictable nature of the job that captured our imaginations. Had I been a boy, I would have considered growing up to work for the state, to set forth with galoshes, muffler and thermos after receiving a midnight call. As a girl, I was content to imagine Mr. Pierson driving through flakes, thinking solitary thoughts in snow.

His work, it seemed to me at the time, rescued him from the ordinary. Pulled him from Mrs. Pierson's cold bed and shrill ways, away from the television that had the widest screen in town and was always playing. He had traded the foreseen for mystery, the housebound travails of other professions such as plumbing or carpentry for the free-ranging vagaries of conquering snow. He was the closest thing we had to a traveler.

The closest thing we had to an explorer. Balboa, Cortez, Perry were lifeless compared with him, had been deadened by fourth grade teachings rendering the events so remote that we failed to experience incredulity that would have aroused our curiosity and inspired admiration. Journeys should not be surrendered to geography teachers.

Before I would teach of Lewis and Clark and Admiral Byrd, I would take my students deep into the woods. Our pockets would contain a few nuts and raisins. We'd carry canteens and wear boots. We would follow the sun. Maybe we would reemerge by dismissal time, maybe not. We would find newts, drink from a stream, rub sticks together to make a fire. The old stick trick wouldn't work, it never does. Those of us who were brave might lift a rock from the forest floor to be amazed and disgusted by the squirming life revealed. We would travel light, curiosity our heaviest load. That's how I like to travel now.

And that's how we traveled as children, on bicycles and horses, exploring new parts of the countryside, packing sandwiches so that there would be no need to return before dark. We were unafraid of losing our way and rather welcomed the prospect.

We probably never covered a radius of more than six miles, but our kingdom seemed boundless, the potential for adventure would not be diminished by all the Saturdays of childhood.

Now that adult perception is in place, and now that six miles don't seem to cover much territory, longer distances are required to recapture the sense of anticipation that anything might happen. One has to travel further to find the country path which, if all goes well, one will get lost upon. One has to venture farther than the snowy night to capture Mr. Pierson's ecstasy—at least Mr. Pierson's ecstasy as we imagined it.

A Visit
to Keats's Grave

"Please do not caress, touch or molest the cats in the Cemetery." Forewarned by these guidelines written in three languages on water-damaged paper, you reach for a rope blackened by time and the tug of many hands. The resulting toll of a bell within the gates brings forth a squinting eye that peers through a peephole. *"Chi è?"* "May we please see the cemetery?" *"Chiuso!"* In Rome, most things at most times are *"chiuso"* (closed). No explanations, no pleading will make the eye relent nor urge a hand to open the fifteen-foot gate above which appear the letters, "Resurrecturis."

As this is the only entrance to the Protestant cemetery, unless you are capable of scaling the ancient Aurelian wall that separates the quick from the dead, you do as you are told and return tomorrow when the gate will open onto cypress, laurel, violets and a kitten sleeping in a cactus leaf. For tonight the graves of Shelley and Keats will remain untouched by the hot fingers of pilgrims.

You are beginning to learn that you cannot call on the dead casually, you cannot call on them at unscheduled times and not in a hurry. The next day, the number 95 bus swoops you off Piazza Venezia, past the Vittorio Emanuele Monument and triumphal arches, past the Capitol's palaces and piazza designed by Michelangelo, along the route of the fallen —the route by which corpses of defeated gladiators and Christian martyrs were removed for burial outside the city walls.

You are dropped at the base of a 140-foot pyramid erected in the first century B.C. as a tomb for Gaius Cestius. According to Thomas Hardy in his poem "Rome: At the Pyramid of Cestius Near the Graves of Shelley and Keats," this tribune of little note achieved a certain immortality "In beckoning pilgrim feet/With marble finger high/To where, by shadowy wall and history-haunted street/Those matchless singers lie. . . ."

So beckoned, you once again make your way to the gates and pray for escape as well as entrance. Out here Fiats, Alfa-Romeos, trucks and motorcycles satisfy the Roman infatuation with the noise of engines and smell of exhaust. They race by buildings as mundane as those on the outskirts of any American town—Columbus, Ohio; New London, Connecticut. None of this was here when Keats chose it as his last resting place, or when Shelley noted in a letter to his friend, Thomas Love Peacock, that it was ". . . the most beautiful and solemn cemetery I ever beheld." At that time no gate separated the cemetery from the surrounding countryside where sheep grazed and Romans picnicked. Now an expressway replaces pasture and automobiles have usurped the sheep.

Yesterday's peering eye is met by its mate and the face of an old man appears before you on the other side of the gate. He wears a newspaper hat, tightly creased and made with care. Above a sunburned left ear appear words from this morning's headlines, *"Prova del voto segreto . . ."* (Proof of the secret vote . . .) He closes the gate after you and departs

in silence with the stooped posture and slow gait of one who
has spent his life tending graves.

Why does one visit such places? It is clear that you feel
closer to Keats when you read the odes, to Shelley as you
reflect on his "Defence of Poetry." Even as you attempt to
stir your still heart by reporting, "Beneath this ground are
the bones of poets, the ashes of a drowned voice," even as
you imagine Shelley's last hours in the tempest immortalized
by lines from Ariel's song engraved on his monument, you
know that you are held at a distance.

Perhaps you come because you too "have been half in
love with easeful Death," have been moved by the age-old
yearning to honor the dead by reading words carved in
stone. You are not alone. Someone has left a pot of pink
petunias on Shelley's grave. They wilt in the heat and need
watering.

A woman arrives with trays of red and white begonias.
Her high heels, kicking up the gravel of the paths, make the
only sound other than the soft tread of cats and the rising
song of evening birds, and yes, nightingales. She kneels before the base of a tombstone bearing the name of a Canadian
man who died last year at the age of twenty-six, and begins to
arrange the plants. She, who might be the mother of the
deceased, is the sole other visitor to this haven behind pyramid and ancient wall, shaded from 4 P.M. sun by fifty-foot
cypress and pine. There is soil on her knees as she stands and
straightens her skirt. "You need to have connections to be
buried here," she says, and wanders off into the shadows of
others' graves.

Of course, in Keats and Shelley's day no connections
were needed. According to Church decree, non-Catholics
were refused burial in consecrated ground, therefore this was
the designated spot, unless one chose to come to rest with
deceased prostitutes near Piazza Flaminia.

As Keats, at the age of twenty-five, lay dying in his small room above the Spanish Steps, he asked Joseph Severn, his friend and deathbed companion, to make a journey to this place in order that he might describe it to him. Keats was pleased to hear that anemones, violets and daisies grew wild among the graves. As death approached he murmured that he could feel "the daisies growing over me."

After the pre-dawn burial that soon followed, Dr. Clark, Keats's devoted physician, directed the gravedigger to put turfs of daisies upon the grave. These have been replaced with violets. And borders of roses, laurel, poppies and bachelor buttons. "All flowers Keats wrote about," a guidebook explains. It seems that few are willing to allow memory and imagination to fill silence and space.

But then, it is not unusual for well-meaning survivors to remove the life from death, to deny its hold on the living. Here they would have it that Keats never longed to relinquish his song to the nightingale. Monuments have been built to rise above his modest and anonymous stone, to admonish this preference for anonymity. Severn's neighboring marker bears the name "John Keats" in letters as large as his own. A monument nearby scolds, "Sleep on! Not honoured less for Epitaph so meek."

Keats's "meek" epitaph was, in essence, his final poem. Conceived as he lay depressed and feverish, hearing the relentless play of water from a Bernini fountain outside his window. These were to be the only words on his tombstone he instructed Severn: "Here lies one whose name was writ in water." He knew that the poem was complete.

But Severn and friends, lacking the poet's ear and sensibility, felt compelled, when the time came, to inscribe an introduction above Keats's epitaph, to explain and misinterpret. The heaviness of their engraved grief and prose appears to weight the top of the stone. "This Grave contains all that was Mortal, of a YOUNG ENGLISH POET, Who, on his Death Bed, in the Bitterness of his Heart at the Malicious

Power of his Enemies, Desired these words to be engraved
on his Tomb Stone . . ."

    If you hold up a hand to block out those words, the
beauty and enigma of Keats's own remain. And poetry takes
care of the rest.

A Visit
with William Faulkner

You half expect him to be there. You begin to sense it the minute telephone information in Oxford, Mississippi, gives you a listing for Rowan Oak, William Faulkner's home. What if the voice at the other end whispers, "Caddy smelled like leaves." Are you ready for that?

In fact, Howard Bahr, the curator answers. He is pleased that there are no tours the day I plan to arrive, that I'll have the place to myself. I ask for directions, are there signs? "Oh no, ma'am. I reckon that's part of the charm."

He directs by bridges and curves. "After the second big curve, north of Oxford, there will be a red gate on the left. There's a large house there in the gully. Park your car and walk up the drive."

The gully turns out to be a grove of maples and oaks at the end of a long cedar-lined drive. You would pass right by that red gate if you had come unalerted. There is no parking lot. Strangers weren't welcomed then and no provision is made for them now.

The April sun is hot, but when you step onto the gravel driveway, the leafy coolness of the cedars chills. These trees

have grown so tall since their planting in 1840, the year the
house was built, that their branches meet some fifty feet overhead as if clasping hands in a stately minuet. About their
bases blue and white irises bloom. Ahead on the left is a
magnolia tree, thirty feet high and at least twenty feet in
girth. Brick walls, laid by the original Scots landscaper, still
meander through azalea, pink and white dogwood, cape jas-
mine, gardenia and gnarled wisteria. An old black man tends
them in silence.

The ear begins to decipher the sounds that make up the
stillness of this place. The persistent buzz of bees and the
general histrionics of mockingbirds. The house comes into
full view. Of course there are pillars, a porch and second-
floor balcony. "Neo-classical," Bahr will tell me. "That's the
way folks like to do."

The heavy front door gives to the turn of a cool knob. A
slight, formal man in his early thirties comes forward.

"Howard Bahr?"

"I am he." He bows slightly from the waist.

"Shall I look around?" I ask, peering ahead at a staircase
fit for a bride's descent.

"By all means, ma'am."

He gestures to the right where a Lucite gate separates us
from a room in which a reading chair poses next to a table
holding an open book and a pipe. This is embarrassing. After
all, Faulkner himself hadn't invited me in. But then I begin to
wonder, what would happen if I leaped over the gate and
took that pipe in my own mouth? I imagine my tongue would
burn. My voice would change. A leftover bit of saliva might
mingle with my own and smite me. Would I smell his hand
on its bowl? His breath on the stem?

"All of this has been left exactly as it was when Mr.
Faulkner died. He wrote in this room when he first moved
here." Bahr's accent is rich and deep. I imagine Mr. Faulkner
would be pleased with the pronunciation—"Mista
FALL'kna." Later, as we get to know each other better, it

becomes, "Mista William," and I suspect that is how Bahr thinks of him.

It is a cool room. Not much sun works its way in here. Books line the shelves beneath a painting of Great-grandpa Colonel W. C. Faulkner, "A heroic sort of fella. He was the model for Colonel Sartoris." And just like the colonel, he was shot and buried beneath a statue of himself looking out over the railroad he started. Bahr's recitation is so natural that it is a moment before I recognize the cadence as Faulkner's own. ". . . his carven eyes gazing out across the valley where his railroad ran, and beyond that, the ramparts of infinity itself."

"Mr. Faulkner's father was also shot, but he survived. Lots of men were shot in those days. Mississippi was a very touchy place. You had to be careful what you said to a fella."

A collection of Byron's poetry bears the old colonel's inscription. "The books here are mostly Mr. Faulkner's. Unfortunately, after he died, his sister-in-law brought over a lot of family books and put them on the shelves. It's taken us a long time to sort out which belonged to him.

"Our philosophy here—by 'our' I mean the people at the university, good, sane men like Dr. Harrington [head of the English Department at Ole Miss]—well, we don't think of it as a museum or a tourist attraction. We think of it as Mr. Faulkner's house. It's in our trust, and we try to run it like a house. I play the piano sometimes and cut flowers. We grow greens. As much as we can, we try to do it like Mr. Faulkner would want it done. It is unique in all the world, probably.

"It ain't Graceland, Elvis Presley's house. They get hundreds of visitors every day and thousands on his birthday. That's all right for old Elvis 'cause that's the way he was. But this place should be quiet and private. So far God and circumstance have made that possible. I think we're doing it the way Mr. Faulkner would like. I say that in all humility."

Ole Miss leased the house immediately after Faulkner's death, and eventually purchased it from his daughter Jill in

1973. The first curator was Dr. James W. Webb. "Dr. Webb. Poor Dr. Webb. How he suffered with the place in the early years. Miss Victoria, Mrs. Faulkner's daughter from her first marriage, came to get what she wanted and the cook was here and Dr. Webb had to stand right over there and watch Miss Victoria give that woman about 80 percent of all the tools and food and things that were in the kitchen. You know how families will do. But this was William Faulkner's stuff and now it's gone forever."

But what remained has been kept as it was, even though this room is not open to the public. Rusting cans of cinnamon, nutmeg and cloves line the spice cupboard.

Similarly, in Mrs. Faulkner's bathroom, which is closed to the public, all has been left as it was found, as if to move a thing would be to disturb the spirits of the place. On the shelf over the sink there are prescription bottles of Seconal and Equanil. Catching my glance, Bahr shakes his head sadly. "Mrs. Faulkner. Well, that's another story. Mrs. Faulkner told Dr. Webb one time, 'I always loved William Faulkner, but I didn't always like him.' They really did love one another, but they were both such volatile people and of course Mr. Faulkner had the burden of his genius. It just couldn't have been any other way."

What brought him here, this young man who approaches the former inhabitants with sympathy and occasional respectful silence? "When I was working on the railroad, a bunch of fellas and I were reading Faulkner. I was twenty-five and reckoned it was time to get some education, so I came up here to Ole Miss to be where Faulkner had been. When Dr. Webb retired, they were kind enough to give me the job. It don't pay a whole lot, but there's no other job in the world I'd rather have. It's a great privilege to be able to have the key to Mr. Faulkner's front door."

He finds that here, "on this Faulkner place, the rhythms of life are kind of like they're supposed to be." Unlike the rest of the world, where "the Snopes are winning. They really are. Do you know that in the McDonald's in town, they have pictures of Faulkner on the walls? Now I wonder what Mista William would say to that."

He thinks for a moment, then lifts a Lucite gate that separates us from the back of the house. "Well, since you've come all this way . . ." and he leads me to a small dark room. This is the office Faulkner added in 1950 after winning the Nobel Prize. It resembles a monk's cell. Unlike the large airy dining room and sitting rooms that open to gardens and afternoon sun, there is a gloom here. Books, a desk, typewriter, cot and on the walls, the outline of *A Fable.* "He worked on that for ten years. The manuscript was all over this floor, so he finally wrote out the action on the walls, to get it straight. We didn't even know that was there until we scraped some paint off." He points to the word "Monday" written in large red letters to the left of the window. Beneath it, Faulkner's precise, penciled printing outlines the plot. The remaining days of the week and the action that occurred on them are written out across the wall above the cot; and then, above its foot, where he must have been able to stare at it from his pillow, is the word, "Tomorrow."

On the way upstairs to the master bedroom, we pass the dining room. "It's feeling out of sorts," says Bahr, nodding toward a leak in the ceiling. There are pink flowers on the table. "Did you arrange those?" I ask. "Yes'm. A house is like a human. If the blood ain't moving in it, it'll die. There's plenty of life goes on here. Plenty of laughter and talkin' and tellin' lies. In the night we'll light up our pipes, drink coffee and tell lies." But he doesn't eat his meals in this room. "I eat in the kitchen. That's only fittin'."

In the bedroom there is a locked wardrobe that holds Faulkner's clothes. These aren't Costume Institute clothes. The life within them has not been starched and ironed out. They are as they were left, and except for today, are kept locked from view. The shoes are small. One pair each: sneakers, riding boots, work boots caked with red Mississippi soil, formal shoes. Each is worn down on the heel in response to the wearer's particular gait and the upper leather bears the imprint of toes, as individual and personal as fingerprints.

And yet, for all this, what is sensed here is not a presence, but a profound absence. Empty space sensed more keenly than that which had previously filled it.

This is even more striking out back, in the pasture. Whereas effects fill the house, no horses graze here. There are no steaming manure piles, no hoof marks captured in mud. The clover rises toward the sun and no teeth claim it.

"Do you ever sense his ghost?" Is that not, after all, what brings us to the homes of the dead? Some faint belief that our own flesh might rub up against the fleshless spirit of one who once lived there?

"No, ma'am. The presence of the past is very strong here, but I think Mr. Faulkner is at rest, and all of his folks. I don't ever feel any presence here but the past itself. I used to live over there in a house beyond the woods. At night, I'd sit out and it would seem that the streams of time were meetin' and flowin' right through that place. This is just a wondrous place and I never get tired of it. Never do.

"You know, we all laugh about sense of place around here, because everybody's always talking about it. Especially up there at the Center for the Study of Southern Culture at the university. But you know, it's true. There is a sense of community and a sense of the land. I don't know what it is. It goes back to the old agrarian ideal. A Jeffersonian love of the land. It's all very complicated, but it all goes back to the heart. I guess it ain't really all that complicated when you get right down to it."

And when you get right down to it, the timelessness here is not in the emptied clothes or pipe, but in the fiction of the man who filled them. It's in this pasture and beneath the giant cedar trees, in the land and the mockingbird's insistent yearning.

A Visit
with Eudora Welty

She's worn a pretty hat for the occasion, an occasion she says she has dreaded ever since the arrangements were made— ever since she decided to make an exception to her rule, no interviews. Her blue eyes draw the visitor through the gate of the Jackson, Mississippi, airport to a cool outstretched hand with fingers so long and slender you know they were made for weaving tales.

The smile is shy, that of an eleven-year-old entering a birthday party where she knows no one, but her mother insisted she come. The voice is soft and hesitant. "You look like a Virginia girl." She reaches for my bag. "No! That's much too heavy." After all, she is seventy-five. Her hair is white. She is slight and walks with slow care in a shiny, brand-new pair of loafers. Her knit dress matches her eyes. The next day, when we have settled into pants, comfortable shoes and friendship, she tells me, "I would have worn pants to the airport, but I thought, 'She'll think I'm some sort of a hick!'"

"You mustn't carry that bag. It's full of books. I don't seem to be able to travel without them." She relaxes and smiles, "Oh, I'm the same way." We both continue to reach for the bag. The one connection between two strangers who want to feel at home. A passion for books. But of course she is at a disadvantage because I am the only stranger here. Her soul has been exposed. "I can't think of any American writer more universally acknowledged to be a great writer," says William Maxwell, her friend and long-time editor at *The New Yorker.* "Everybody—every *cat* knows that Eudora Welty is a great writer."

She eases herself behind the wheel of her car. She can barely see over it. She's tired. "I've been on the go ever since the first of the year. And this weekend I signed four hundred of those Harvard books for a limited edition. Are you going to want to use a tape recorder? I always think I sound as if I don't know what I'm talking about when I'm on tape. You'll have to excuse me if I don't hear you. I don't hear as well as I used to." The words come slowly.

The "Harvard books" refers to her autobiographical *One Writer's Beginnings.* That it is a bestseller, "is just some sort of freak," she says. Based on lectures she gave at the university, "It was the hardest thing I've ever had to do. First there were the lectures. I don't know why they wanted me. I'm no scholar and I hate to lecture. I much prefer conversation—a back and forth exchange. I've always had to teach to supplement my income, but I think if I had it to do again, I'd do something completely different. Not different than writing. Different than teaching. I think I'd do something mechanical. Something with my hands."

"Such as plumbing?"

"Such as painting chairs. You paint a chair in the morning, and there it is in the afternoon." Her hand strokes an imaginary armrest.

She sighs, "And then I had to rewrite the lectures for the book." A book that, according to Maxwell, "We are so lucky to have. The material is so private for her. It might not seem private to other people. That she was willing to part with it is extraordinary." Just how extraordinary becomes increasingly apparent over the next few days as the more she reveals of herself, the more she reveals her passion for privacy. Writing *One Writer's Beginnings* was a constant struggle between that passion and her conscience. She would do the job she set out to do.

"It was amazing to discover that *nothing* is ever lost. Thomas Mann was right, the memory is a well. In writing this book each memory uncovered another. It was probably important for me to remember these things, but it was very hard."

Hard to reminisce about the premature deaths of her father and two brothers to whom she was very close. Hard to delve into her mother's depression. "I kept thinking, 'If *only* I'd known then what I know now.' Or, 'If only I'd said . . .' And I'm so sorry I never had a chance to tell my father how I felt about him. We were a very reserved family. But *passionate.*"

As is its remaining survivor. She believes that letters should be burned, journals never commenced and biographies left unwritten. At the same time she has a strong identification with her character Miss Eckhart, the piano teacher of whom she wrote in "June Recital," "Coming from Miss Eckhart, the music made all the pupils uneasy, almost alarmed, something had burst out, unwanted, exciting, from the wrong person's life."

Similarly, in her art she has "offered, offered, offered"; just as Miss Eckhart "offered Virgie her Beethoven." But Miss Welty insists that the offering to the public should be limited to the art. "It's not that there would be any 'disclosures'—that's what seems to sell biographies these days—disclosures. I don't have anything to conceal. It's not that I have bastard children running around." She rolls her eyes and laughs at the thought. "It's just that my life is private. I really think Faulkner was right. If you want to know about a writer, read his fiction."

In her review of the published letters of William Faulk-

ner edited by Joseph Blotner, she wrote, "No man ever put
more of his heart and soul into the written word than did
William Faulkner. If you want to know all you can about that
heart and soul, the fiction where he put it is still right there.
The writer offered it to us from the start and when we didn't
even want it or know how to take it and understand it; it's
been there all along and is more likely to remain. Read that."

She could be writing about herself. So it should come as
no surprise that in *One Writer's Beginnings* part of that self
remains in shadow; that even at times of great emotion she
remains at her "private remove." Of her father's death and
the blood transfusion that was a desperate attempt to avert it,
she writes:

> I was present when it was done; my two broth-
> ers were in school. Both my parents were lying on
> cots, my father had been brought in on one and my
> mother lay on the other. Then a tube was simply
> run from her arm to his . . .

> All at once his face turned dusky red all over.
> The doctor made a disparaging sound with his lips,
> the kind a woman makes when she drops a stitch.
> What the doctor meant by it was that my father was
> dead.

What is left unwritten is how she felt. "I originally had it
in the book, but I took it out. I thought it would be too self-
indulgent. What I remember is that there were venetian
blinds in back of me. That the heat of the sun was coming
through the slats and onto my back. I suppose that was my
creeping horror. That's what a person remembers—the physical sensation. I'd never seen anyone die before. Have you?"

She often asks such questions. "Don't you?" "Can you
imagine?" "Don't you find that to be true?" It is her attempt
to bring you into the circle. To include you. For all the re-

serve, she invites you to draw near, to be comfortable. It goes
beyond Southern hospitality. It is a complete turning over of
the self to another's sensibilities. "Are you warm enough?"
"Are you hungry yet?" "Land! You shouldn't have spent so
much money on that book. I would have given you a copy."
"I worry about you."

Since it is not possible to capture on paper the rich melody of her accent, it is best to try to visualize sound, to keep
in mind an aerial view of the Mississippi River. Soft and
deep, with slow rhythmic twists and turns. The inflections.
The asides. She says that she learned from her good friend
Faulkner "to use punctuation rather than phony dialect to
reveal how a person sounds." But at the risk of slipping into
dialect, I think you should know that "marvelous," a word
she uses often, is pronounced "MAHvelus"; that it comes
from deep within the throat in a slow savoring of the object
admired.

There are also certain words that should only be spoken
by Eudora Welty. "Buzzard" and "sinister" are two of these.
As we drive along the Natchez Trace, the setting of many of
her tales, two of the above-mentioned birds are spotted
weighing down branches atop a dead tree. "Buzzuds!" She
shudders, "I hate buzzuds! I always knew, when I was coming home on a train, when we had entered Mississippi because you would see buzzuds out the window."

When we drive off the highway to visit a cypress swamp,
her whisper breaks through our daydreaming. "Isn't it
sinista?" I feel that on her tongue I heard for the first time all
that is ominous in those two words.

It is hard to tell as we travel along the Trace how much is
truly "sinista" and how much is Eudora Welty mocking her
own imagination. "We mustn't get far from the highway,"
she warns. "Scary things still happen here. Just as they did in
the days of the outlaws." She is smiling at the same time that
she arranges her face in an expression of fear, like a parent
telling a child a bedtime story. She chills me with the true

history of the Trace, the land route followed by merchants after reaching the head of navigation in the Mississippi. "They were robbed of their gold and murdered all the time. . . .

"This," she says sadly, pointing to swamps appearing on either side of the highway and trees meeting above it, "This is what it all used to look like." And that is why she has brought me to this place. "I have never seen, in this small section of old Mississippi River country and its little chain of lost towns between Vicksburg and Natchez, anything so mundane as ghosts, but I have felt many times there a sense of place as powerful as if it were visible and walking and could touch me." ("Some Notes on River Country.")

This is the country traveled and photographed when she was a publicity agent for the WPA during the depression. The click of the shutter secured in the recesses of her mind these scenes and those who inhabited the "lost towns." Later when she turned to stories, they formed the persona and landscapes of "A Worn Path," "Asphodel," "Livvie," "At the Landing," *Losing Battles.*

Because *this* is what we think of as Eudora Welty country, it is jarring to leave the Trace and drive into Jackson, a city of 300,000. Up 297,000 since her parents settled here as a young married couple—her father from a farm in Ohio and her mother from the mountains of West Virginia. The grand homes that once graced State Street have given way to Cooke's Prosthetics and Cash-in-a-Flash Pawn Shop. The architecture is that of any town in commercial, suburban America. "I used to play in all these yards," she says, pointing to parking lots. "And that is where the insane asylum used to be. Imagine. 'Lunatic Asylum' was carved on the gateway. That's what they were talking about in *The Sound and the Fury* when they would say they were going to send Benjy to Jackson. In those days Jackson meant the loony bin."

Her own street, back from State, is quiet and slightly elevated. Her father chose the site in part to ease her moth-

er's homesickness. But "my mother never could see the hill."
Her childhood home, a 1920's Tudor-style designed by her
father, is solid and graceful. "I feel awfully selfish living here
alone, and I can't afford to keep it up the way I should. But,"
she shrugs helplessly, "I can't imagine moving. And it's
home." The lawn is full of pine needles and is dominated by
a huge oak tree. "The builder told my parents to chop down
that tree, but they said, 'Never chop down an oak tree.' They
were country people. I guess that was something country
people say. Well, they were right. That's the only one left.
Most of the pines have died."

We enter through a vestibule. "My father was a Yankee.
He thought *all* houses should have vestibules." There is a
living room to the left and a library to the right. Between is a
solid mahogany staircase built for the ages. And everywhere
there are books. Books by close friends: Walker Percy, Reynolds Price, Elizabeth Bowen, Katherine Anne Porter, Elizabeth Spencer, William Jay Smith and Robert Penn Warren.
The diaries of Virginia Woolf, a new biography of Ford Madox Ford. "I am fascinated by the time he encompassed. Can
you imagine that he held a chair for Turgenev!" Seamus He-
aney, Barbara Pym, Chekhov and all of Henry Green, one of
her favorites. They've overrun bookshelves and have moved
to tables and desks.

On the mantel is a Snowden photograph of V. S. Pritch-
ett looking spry and amused in his eighties. She cut it from a
magazine and mounted it. "Isn't he a dream boy?" The coy
tilt of the head, the pleasure in the smile conjure an image of
the sixteen-year-old Eudora sharing news about a boy in town
with her friend Charlotte Capers (who still lives nearby and is
still a friend). A similar photo is on her desk. "For inspira-
tion."

The desk is in the bedroom where she works as she did
from the beginning. "When there were five of us here, it was
the only place I *could* work," she says, referring to the days
when her parents and brothers also occupied this house.

She is generous in her praise and encouragement of other writers. It appears that her life is free of jealousy—personal or professional. She wishes others well and delights in their successes. "Anne Tyler was a whiz from the time she was seventeen!" She laughs as she recalls, "Reynolds [Price] had Anne for one of his first students. He thought, 'Teaching is going to be great!' He thought *all* his students were going to be like Anne." She thinks the title of Tyler's novel, *Dinner at the Homesick Restaurant* "is inspired," and that the last sentence is a tour de force. "If I had written that sentence, I'd be happy all my life!"

When it is mentioned that she has written some rather galvanizing sentences herself, and that "Keela, the Outcast Indian Maiden" is no less than an inspired title, she merely responds, "Well, you're sweet to say so." Modesty is something you are not going to budge in this lady. It's as firmly rooted as that oak standing there beyond the windows.

When asked about another prize-winning writer whose work she has reviewed, she says, "I wanted so much to like her book but I found some of it impossibly precious. I did not put my misgivings in the review because it was the first book by a young writer and I couldn't hurt somebody like that. She was a bit self-indulgent, which is *perfectly natural* for someone of that much talent. I tried to point out the parts that I thought were marvelous."

"[Miss Eckhart's] love never did anybody any good," she writes in "June Recital." It is impossible to think that Miss Welty's love has not done many a young writer a great deal of good.

As much as she enjoys talking of writers and books, she positively beams when speaking of the act of writing itself. "I love the *function* of writing—what it is *doing.*" She offers to pour us some Jack Daniel's. "What Katherine Anne Porter called 'suich licour.' Just a jigger. This is powerful stuff. Whenever Robert Penn Warren is coming he calls and says, 'Eudora, get out the Black Jack, I'm comin' to town.' " Mississippi nights are cold at this time of the year, the bourbon is comforting and we settle in to talk of her favorite subject.

"Elizabeth Bowen in her marvelous notes on writing a novel in her book *Collected Impressions* pointed out that dialogue is really a form of action. Because it advances the plot. It's not just chatter. She was so succinct in what she said. I think television may have ruined that for us. If you watch serials and talk shows, you would probably think that one-liners were the answer to conversation. That is what has hurt Broadway so; dialogue has been sacrificed for the one-liner. That's putting it too extremely, but the building of a conversation is to gradually reveal something.

"Elizabeth was a marvelous writer about writing and very helpful to me. So was E. M. Forster's *Aspects of the Novel.* I don't think that can ever be outdated. It's important to read these books, but you can't teach a person how to write. That has to come directly from inside the writer.

"What I try to show in fiction are the truths of human relationships. But you have to make up the lies of fiction to reveal these truths—people interacting; things beginning one way and changing to reveal something else. You *show* a truth. You don't tell it. It has to be done of itself."

She feels the same way about moralizing in fiction. "A writer has to have a strong moral sense. You couldn't write if you yourself didn't have it and know what you were doing. But that's very different than wanting to moralize in your story. Your own moral sense tells you what's true and false and how people would behave. And you know what is just and unjust, but you don't point them out. In my view. I don't think it works in fiction because fiction is dramatic. It's not a platform.

"That worried me in the sixties because I was asked so many times by strangers why I didn't come out for civil rights, something I'd worked for for years. They would call me in the middle of the night, mostly from New Jersey and New York City. They would say, 'Eudora Welty, what are you doing down there sitting on your *ass?*' I just told them that I knew what I could write and what I couldn't. That I was doing the best I could in my own field. I would be so shaken up that I couldn't sleep the rest of the night." Now her phone number is unlisted.

We empty our glasses and depart for dinner at Bill's Burger House. Burgers by day, native red fish by night. She is welcomed more like a football captain of a local, undefeated team than a literary eminence. Bill grabs her hand and tells me with Greek-accented gusto, "Everybody love this charming lady." And for final flourish, "God Bless America!"

A pretty young woman approaches our table. "Miss Welty, you honored us by gracing our wedding tea. I just wanted to say hello." After she leaves I'm told whom she married. The parents and grandparents are identified, as are the members of the family who are Yankees. I begin to understand what she meant when she said that she agreed with Walker Percy's comment to reporters that the reason the South had so many fine writers was, "Because we lost." She elaborates, "Since we never really industrialized—reconstruction saw to that—the pace is slower. People don't move around as much. You know who a person's mother is. We're more introspective, interested in the psychology of people."

The next morning when we meet she shares the mail with me, mail that keeps her awake at night because "I feel so guilty that I never have time to answer it." This morning's correspondence includes a letter from sixteen-year-old Christine from Georgia, who writes, "I really loved 'Why I Live at the P.O.' because it is so true to life. My brother and sister are always trying to get me in trouble." Then she asks whether the narrator of the story "will come back home, and do you think her parents will take her in if she does?"

"Christine doesn't know it yet, but she's fixin' to leave," Miss Welty muses. Well, what about her question? Will the character return? The character who swore, "But here I am, and here I'll stay. I want the world to know I'm happy."

"Of course." The answer is as natural as though we were speaking of a flesh and blood neighbor. "These people *live* by dramatizing themselves. She'll come home, they'll take her in, and it will start all over again."

Her only response to news of a published paper that compares "Why I Live at the P.O." to Homer and the Bible is, "Can you *imagine?*" She is equally horrified by letters from students who ask whether the apple eaten by the girl who has visited the Old Ladies Home in "A Visit of Charity" is the apple from the Garden of Eden. "The things some teachers teach! She was just eating that the way you would a Hershey Bar—or anything else you'd saved for a reward after an ordeal. I used to visit the old ladies. They scared me. I couldn't wait to leave and I'm sure they couldn't wait to have me leave."

There are letters asking for explanations. "I think that bears a lot on the fact that young people—students and children—are not taught and don't understand the difference between fiction and nonfiction. I recently heard about a student who, having found my name in a directory, said to his teacher, 'It says here that Miss Welty lives on Pinehurst. I thought she lived at the post office.' Well, after all," she says, pretending this is perfectly understandable, " 'Why I Live at the P.O.' *was* written in the first person.

"They are not taught. They don't experience what a story does. They just try to *figure it out.* Again, I think that television has something to do with it. People don't believe events. I remember when man landed on the moon, I called my cleaning woman in to watch it on television, 'You should see this,' I told her. And she said, 'Now, Miss Eudora, you know that ain't true.' "

She tells of a phone call received shortly after publication of *The Ponder Heart,* "The funniest book ever written by a human being," according to William Maxwell. "The phone rang and a voice said, 'Miss Welty?' 'Yes?' 'This is Officer Ponder.' He was a policeman. 'I'm standing on the corner of Capitol and Congress. I understand you've written a history of my family.' I explained to him, 'Mr. Ponder, that was a story. I love my characters. But they are not real.' Ponder. Isn't that a wonderful name? So he said, 'Oh. Well. If you ever need me I'm here at the corner of Capitol and Congress.' "

That her characters have names similar to or the same as her neighbors' is no accident. "It must always be a name that people really name their children." Even when that name is chosen for mythological significance. "Of course I knew what that meant when I named Phoenix Jackson, but it was also a name that was common among old black women. White owners often gave their slaves mythological names, so we have lots of Homers and Ulysses and Parthenias. Also, poor people in the South tend to give their children beautiful names. They think, 'Well, at least I can give her a pretty name.' And they do."

Asked about Old Man Fate Rainey in *The Golden Apples,* she says, "The South is full of Fates. It turns out to be short for Lafayette who was a real hero down here." And Miss Ice Cream Rainey? "I learned that in Wales they give people names like Tree-Chopper Jones to distinguish him from the other Joneses. My dancing school teacher was called Miss Ice Cream McNair because her husband owned the ice cream parlor. Of course we never called her that to her face."

In a sense these names are found poetry. From obituaries, the telephone book, memory, bus rides and conversation come Old Mrs. Sad-Talking Morgan, Miss Billy Texas Spights, Mr. Fatty Bowles, Stella-Rondo, Homer Champion, Miss Snowdie MacLain. All characters existing in the nimbus of Welty's love.

"She dotes on them," says Maxwell.

"I loved all my schoolteachers. And I loved everybody in *The Golden Apples.* The good ones and the bad. The happy

ones and the sad ones. I loved them all." Conversation returns to Phoenix Jackson, the elderly black woman in "A
Worn Path," who makes death-defying trips to town for her
grandson's medicine, "I worried about her so much," I say.
Welty sighs, "I still do."

Of course there is the famous exception—the character
she created out of anger rather than love the night that
Medgar Evers was shot. The similarity was so striking between the arrested suspect and the imagined murderer, the
narrator of "Where Is the Voice Coming From?" that
changes had to be made before the story appeared in *The
New Yorker*. "There was concern that it would be like convict-
ing him before the trial. Of course I didn't know him. I just
knew the type of person who might do that and I got inside
his head." The title was chosen because she "really did not
know where the voice was coming from that was telling the
story."

"I think writers hallucinate," Maxwell suggests. "I'm
nothing but a pen," said Jean Rhys. "I don't know where it
came from. I don't know why God or gods, or whoever it
was, selected me to be the vessel. Believe me, this is not
humility, false modesty; it is simply amazement," William
Faulkner wrote to Joan Williams. Eudora Welty shares the
amazement and has no answer to the mystery.

"It's so queer. Your material guides you and enlightens
you along the way. That's how you find out what you were
after. It *is* a mystery. When I'm not writing, I can't *imagine*
writing. And when I am writing, it doesn't occur to me to
wonder. Sometimes I feel like a completely split personality.
I think the really true self is probably the one that is writing.
But the other self is trying to protect me. Sometimes I think,
'While I'm out at the grocery store will be a good time for
me to retype this.' That is, that my daily life will leave me
alone to do my work." She pauses to consider this, then
laughs shyly, "They're really going to think I've lost my marbles if you print that."

She speaks of other aspects of the work. "Your ears
should be like magnets. I used to be able to hear people in
back and in front of me and on the street. I don't hear as
much as I used to. It's so *maddening* not to hear overheard
remarks. I hate that. When you're working on a story it's
always with you. You hear somebody say something and you
know that that is what one character is going to say to another."

One such overheard remark gave birth to "Death of a
Traveling Salesman." She writes of the experience in *One
Writer's Beginnings.* "My first good story began spontane-
ously, in a remark repeated to me by a traveling man—our
neighbor—to whom it had been spoken while he was on a
trip into north Mississippi; 'He's gone to borry some fire.'
The words, which carried such lyrical and mythological and
dramatic overtones, were real and actual . . ." Today she
says with fresh wonder, "Who could hear that and not tingle
all over?"

Given this degree of responsiveness, who can resist
bringing her a gift of something overheard? Reynolds Price
recently came bearing what she considers a treasure. "Reynolds was coming here from the airport in a taxi. He said that
the driver told him that the reason the reservoir keeps flood-
ing is because, 'That dam is done eat out by crawfish.' Isn't
that marvelous! 'Done eat out by crawfish.' "

Eager to play, I share an absurdity observed earlier in
the day. "Maybe you could use it," I jest. "Or it could use
me," is her serious response. And that is the point. She is
willing to be used by whatever would become art.

And of course there is the eye. "The fictional eye sees in,
through, and around what is really there," she writes in the
new book. And yet, once that eye has seen and reported its
observation, we see that it *is* really there, and wonder, how
did we miss it? As she and I stood staring into the silent
gloom of the cypress swamp I asked her, "How would you
describe that color?" I was referring to the water's strange

shade of beige beneath the darker brown of tree shadows. "Oh, sort of blue. Like an ink wash." Blue? Ink wash? What was she talking about? Where was she looking? And suddenly there it was. It was everywhere and had been there all the while. She had seen the color of the air.

There's an epidemic with 27 million victims. And no visible symptoms.

It's an epidemic of people who can't read.

Believe it or not, 27 million Americans are functionally illiterate, about one adult in five.

The solution to this problem is you... when you join the fight against illiteracy. So call the Coalition for Literacy at toll-free **1-800-228-8813** and volunteer.

**Volunteer
Against Illiteracy.
The only degree you need
is a degree of caring.**

Ad Council Coalition for Literacy